# VISCOUNT OF VICE

## LORDS OF SCANDAL BOOK 4

TAMMY ANDRESEN

*Keep up with all the latest news, sales, freebies, and releases by joining my newsletter!*

*www.tammyandresen.com*

*Hugs!*

# CHAPTER ONE

LORD BLAKELY EVERBEE, The Viscount of Viceroy, sat next to Miss Ada Chase as they both watched her cousin walk down the aisle toward his friend, The Earl of Exmouth. He grimaced, flexing his fingers. Vice bloody hated weddings. And he especially despised them while sitting next to an eligible woman who, if he wasn't mistaken, was going to cry.

He nearly spit as he spied the little drop of water forming in the corner of her eye. Then she did what all ladies did. With a delicate dab of her kerchief, she let out a small sigh. The sort that might lull a man into going soft. "Isn't this just beautiful?"

Vice had to confess that while the wedding itself was dreadful, the sight of her wasn't terribly awful. It was rather nice, in fact.

He didn't dare credit her with any more than nice, however. He was considered by most to be exceptionally handsome, his features near angelic. And he held the women he dallied with to very high standards. They were the most beautiful, talented, gifted, or accomplished women in England and wider Europe for that manner. He'd had an affair, for example, with a gypsy known for her ability to read cards with deadly accuracy and drink vodka with the best men.

He'd carried on with the most famous actress in all of London, been with a Russian princess who was rich beyond his wildest imaginings. All in all, the list of women he'd shared a bed with was an accomplishment in and of itself. One he was proud of.

And Miss Ada wasn't list-worthy. Yes, she was lovely with her pale auburn hair glimmering in the sun and her bright green eyes that only appeared more sparkly with the sheen of tears. And yes, her figure was supple, the perfect amount of soft curves with an ample bosom and a tiny waist. Of course, her trembling lip as she stared at the bride and groom made him wonder what she might taste like. And the tiny noise of satisfaction she emitted sounded like the sweetest pillow talk he'd ever heard. But Miss Chase wasn't accomplished at anything of significance…and therefore was not his sort at all.

"That kiss." She turned toward him, her eyes a bit dreamy, her head tilted to one side. "Diana is glowing."

Vice's mouth twisted into a frown. "Glowing?" His mouth tasted like he'd eaten gravel. Why did women insist on being so naively romantic? That was another trait most women he dallied with decidedly lacked. They did not understand the world for the harsh place it was.

Ada tapped his arm with her fan. A light touch that made the fabric of his waistcoat brush against his arm with a bit of tickle. "Don't you see it? The color in her cheeks. Her breathless smile. It's just—"

"Beautiful?" Vice filled in the word she'd just used moments before. His voice held disdain rather than dewy-eyed optimism. "You've already told us."

She angled toward him then, her mouth slightly parted, her eyes crinkling at the corners. "You don't think so?"

He assessed her features. Her high cheekbones were flushed with a pinkish brown hue that accentuated the tiny spattering of freckles across her nose. They were not to his usual taste at all, giving her an air of innocence, but he found he'd like to count them. Perhaps kiss a few. "Weddings are generally a bore. And even worse, all I can think is that the groom has given up all the fun in life to take care of a woman and a parcel of brats that are soon to follow."

Ada sniffed, turning back toward the front. "My goodness, you are dreadful, aren't you?"

His best friend, the Baron of Baderness, sat two seats away, next to Ada's cousin, Lady Grace. Now Grace was a woman that might make his list. The features of her face were a perfect mask of feminine beauty. Her thick, pale blonde hair was artfully arranged to highlight her high cheekbones with their perfect pink coloring. Bad leaned over, making eye contact despite the two ladies between them. "He's beyond dreadful. I might use the word insufferable," Bad murmured just loud enough for the four of them to hear him.

Grace giggled. "You're quite funny. You're usually so quiet, I didn't realize you had a sense of humor." That made Bad snap his mouth shut and sit back in his chair.

It was Vice's turn to chuckle. "He isn't. He only makes a joke once every five years."

Ada's mouth curved into a small grin. The sort where her lips stayed together, not showing any of her teeth. But she shook her head, as though she disapproved despite her relaxed features. Then one finger came to her chin. "Insufferable?" She looked back at him, her green eyes sparkling. "The word suits you."

He cocked a brow. By his estimation, Ada Chase had no right to give him any trouble at all. Six weeks prior, she, her sister, and their cousins, had entered into his secret gaming hell that he ran with five of his friends. They'd learned the men's secret and put themselves in danger. Now, he and Bad were being forced to babysit the only two Chase women who weren't wed. They needed to keep his secret and he needed to make certain they were safe. A mad woman named Lady Abernath had been terrorizing the Chase women to expose Vice and his friends. The job was worse than attending this wedding.

"And what word might suit you?" He returned, leaning closer. Which might have been a mistake. She smelled of cookies or cinnamon. Perhaps both. No wait, he caught subtle whiffs of honey laced into her sweet smell. Without meaning to, he drew in a deep whiff. Delightful.

She shrugged but her face tensed and she clasped her hands in her lap. Dropping her head to look down at them, she pursed her lips. "Am I to insert the word most often used to describe me?"

"If it pleases you." He sat back feeling as though

he'd just won some unnamed battle of wits. He could see her discomfort.

Then she relaxed. Her head drew higher as the lines of her body straightened. Ada looked over at him, leaning close. "My sister and cousins often call me little bird. I suppose it's because I tend to flit with nervousness."

That sounded about right to him. Looking at her features now, she was just as beautiful, if not more so than Grace. But she lacked the confidence that drew attention to those looks. Why would a woman as beautiful as her not see her own value?

She pressed a bit closer still and her left breast brushed against his arm. His entire body clenched at the light touch as her breath whispered across the skin of his ear, near causing him to shiver. There was nothing mousy about that move. "But in the last year, I've gotten a new nickname."

He turned to her then, realizing just how close she was, an inch, perhaps two, and he could press his lips to her softly parted ones. He fisted his fingers to keep from caressing her face. Damn he wanted to kiss her. How did she manage to entice an experienced rake like him? "What is it?"

"Ruiner of rakes," she answered, looking him directly in the eye. "Can you imagine a sillier name?"

Was she moving closer? He blinked twice trying to make his eyes work properly when she straightened away again. "You? Ruiner of rakes? I've met some women in my day who could claim that title, but you? A woman capable of making a sinful man repent?"

She gave a tiny shrug. She didn't pull away but he did notice a tiny crinkling about the eyes, almost as though she were wincing. "I know. It's absurd really."

He narrowed his gaze. Was she challenging him? His mouth curved into a smile as a new idea caught his fancy. If she wanted to wage a war in the field of affection, he was game. And if she really did have a reputation as a reformer of rakes, well, she'd make a nice addition to his list.

Having her attention would help accomplish another goal as well. In fact, his job would be far easier if she wished to be by his side. He'd agreed to keep watch over her when she was in public. It was the reason he sat next to her today. Ada had discovered a secret about his friends and he needed to make certain she kept that secret. And recent events dictated that he also keep her safe.

A tiny voice niggled in the back of his thoughts that he was as bad as his mother had claimed him to be. But he pushed that thought aside. He was helping her. That much was certain and he wouldn't go so far as to actually ruin her reputation. The game was harmless. Better than harmless, it helped to keep her safe.

He gave her his most charming smile. "Not absurd at all. I see it now. Your hair reminds me of sunset on a warm summer day and your eyes are the color of new grass. How could a rake not be enchanted?"

Rather than smile, she grimaced, her lips sweet lips turning down into a decided frown. "I don't know what you're playing at but it won't work with me."

He started, which pushed him toward the edge of his chair, and his back slipped off the narrow strip of wood it had been leaning against. He was never clumsy and he didn't understand it now, but in sickening slow motion, he fell to the side, catching his hand on the very piece of wood that had just failed him. The problem was that his weight had shifted to one side of the seat, at least that was what he decided later. In the moment, however, he careened off to one side, both him and the chair crashing to the ground. Gasps filled the air as the organ came to a grinding halt. He looked up to find Ada staring at him as though he'd grown a second head.

———

ADA LOOKED at the Viscount laying at her feet, tangled in his chair. She nibbled at her lip trying to decipher the gravity of the situation.

First, she'd just lied through her teeth. No one in the history of the world had ever considered her a *ruiner of rakes*. It was a complete falsehood. In fact, they often teased her for being bland and frightened by everything, men especially. She wasn't sure why they scared her so. They were a mystery to her when everyone else seemed to understand them so perfectly. Diana, for example, understood exactly how to make a man do what she wanted him to do precisely when she wished him to do it.

But Ada went silent every time a handsome man spoke to her. Twice, she'd tripped on her own feet when one had asked her to dance, and once, she'd managed to push her partner into the punch bowl. It was the most humiliating scene of her life. Well, except for right now. She wasn't certain how, but she surely was to blame for his spill onto the floor.

But worse than the falsehood she'd just told was that her lie had clearly discombobulated the Viscount and once he realized she'd fibbed, well he'd be even angrier. Men were usually furious when she tripped them or sent them flying into the punch. Ada never got away with falsehoods. Some people could, but not her. Diana swore that every lie was visible on her face. It must be true. How else did she get caught every time?

And she was certain he already suspected the lie. Hadn't he said so when he'd told her that he'd known women who could carry the title of rake ruiner? She was certain he had. And implied in that statement were two facts she'd long known about herself. One, she was not that sort of woman at all. Her past had underscored that fact over and over. And two, a man like the Viceroy would never be interested in her. He'd all but said the words himself. Which was likely why she didn't stumble all over herself in his presence. She'd been able to talk and she hadn't tripped him once. Until now, of course.

"Lord Viceroy, are you all right?" She reached down as the entire wedding party stopped to stare at them. He took her hand but was too tangled in the chair to get up.

Standing, she righted the wooden seat and then reached down for Lord Viceroy again. Wedged in a small aisle, she meant to help him stand with as much dignity as possible. But he pulled before Ada had planted her feet. Rather than helping him stand, she toppled forward landing directly on him, her face nearly smashing into his. He stuck his hand between them, which was a good thing. If he hadn't, their teeth might very well have crashed together but his knuckle hit her cheekbone and a sharp pain made her roll to the side.

"Ouch," she cried.

He wrapped his other arm about her, just managing to keep her from crashing into the chairs while she planted one hand on the floor next Viceroy's face, the other pressing to his chest. Moving his hand, he cupped her cheek and turned her face. "Damn it all to hell," he muttered. "You're going to have a bruise."

She tried to scramble off his body, but her skirts had gotten tangled from her movement on top of him. Her legs wound about his and their hips pressed together. All the contact…well…it heated her blood. Or was that her embarrassment? No, she was used to that emotion and this was definitely more. She'd never touched a man like this before and he was so muscular underneath her. A pulse began to ache between her legs. So handsome…

Her breath caught and her eyes widened. Could he tell how she was responding? He was still studying her cheek. "Daring is going to kill me," he muttered under his breath.

"It's not your faul—"

As if he'd heard, Ada's brother-in-law, the Duke of Darlington, called from two rows back. "What is going on up there?"

Ada pressed her lips together. Daring, as Vice called Darlington, was her sister's husband. But he was also one of Vice's good friends and they owned the club together along with the Marquess of Malicorn, Earl of Exmouth, and the Baron of Baderness.

"It's fine," she called back as if that made everything all right. At least Vice didn't appear terribly angry. "We'll be up in just a moment. No need to worry."

"Bloody hell," Vice said, his normally pleasant features twisting into a frown.

The man had blond hair with sky-blue eyes, chiseled features, and full lips. Her breath caught again as her hand fisted in his shirt. Which only served to remind her how strong and hard his chest was.

Vice sat up and somehow managed to pull her up with him, climbing to his feet while holding her. He set Ada back on the floor, his hands firmly on her waist. "My apologies for falling. Thank you for attempting to help me. I did not intend to pull you…"

She waved her hand. Was he apologizing to her?

"The fault was most assuredly mine." Then she took a step back, nearly tripping on Grace's feet. Why did she get so flustered?

Her parents had turned back to stare and Ada wished she could disappear into the floor. Everyone stared. She wobbled and Vice's hands shot out to hold her in place again. Her skin shivered at his touch. He gave her another charming grin. The sort that looked practiced and false. Her shivers stopped. He made her weak in the knees but not when he looked so rehearsed. That look reminded her that she was one of many women he'd charmed, and likely the least of them. The heaviness that made her limbs clumsy, disappeared. She did not want this man any more than he wanted her.

"If you insist on taking the blame, I won't stop you." Then he winked.

She narrowed her eyes as she cocked her head to the side, assessing him. When they'd been tangled together on the floor, she'd forgotten what sort of man he was. For a moment, he was just the handsome, well-built man pressed against her. And honestly, she did respond to him in ways she didn't fully understand. But when he started talking... He made her angry, first and foremost. Most likely because she knew a man like him would never actually be interested in her. At least not after she knocked him to the ground a few more times. He'd run away as fast as his feet could carry him. His stock lines were meant for any woman with a pulse. He didn't recognize her disdain, of course, but Ada was well acquainted with men like Vice.

She knew what sort she'd marry. An affable fellow that her sister would likely call dull. Sure, Minnie and Diana had tamed rakes but Ada, she'd be lucky to tame her red hair into a coif subdued enough for a merchant or a doctor. She'd been courted by an adventurer. Or that's what she liked to call him. A man who went off to exciting places to study animals. But even he'd left her. She just wasn't exciting enough, she was certain of it. Her chest tightened and her head dropped. A clumsy, boring woman. That's what she was. "You do know that gentleman take the blame as a rule."

"I'm no gentleman," he whispered leaning close. "But if you'd like me to, it can be all my fault. This time and every time."

Every time? What was that supposed to mean? She scrunched her brow but his wicked grin that curled his lips told her that he meant something untoward and was now making fun of her lack of experience.

There was no point in answering, so she sat

down, her gaze straight ahead so as not to have to look at anyone. The wedding had ended and the rosy feeling that had filled her chest watching the nuptials was gone. Which was all Vice's fault. Crossing her arms, she glared at him. She might hate that man.

# CHAPTER TWO

ADA WAS nothing like he'd expected from their first meeting. She'd been soft, compliant as far as he could tell. He'd assumed that gaining her affection would be as easy as giving her a few kind words.

Her glare, currently burning into his chest, said otherwise. Still, he liked a challenge. And Ada was all the more interesting for being less pliant.

Now, gaining her affection would not only make his life easier, it would make it all the more fun.

But a niggle of doubt crept into his thoughts. What if Ada was like Camille? A woman of worth who found him to be worthless? He flinched, remembering her. He'd spent years attempting to prove her wrong.

He shook his head. He'd not allow his relation-ship with Ada to go that far. He just wanted her to have a small crush, that would enable him to more easily watch over her. Of course, he didn't want her to get too close. He never allowed any of them to get really close. Not since Camille.

He met her eyes, hers narrowing with irritation.

Giving her his best smile, he righted his chair and then reached out his hand. "Shall we go greet the bride and groom?"

She drew in a long breath before gingerly placing hers in his. "Let's."

Her mother leaned over from the row in front of them. "Are you all right, Ada?"

Ada gave a stiff nod. "Fine, mother."

Her mother gave Vice a quick glance, before leaning over to whisper. "You must try to be more ladylike. I don't know why this keeps—"

Ada huffed, embarrassment making her cheeks heat. "I was perfectly ladylike. There is no need to further my humiliation."

Her mother wrinkled her brow, snapping her fan against her palm. "Ada Lynn." Her voice came out sharp, rising to echo through the church. "I've raised you to be more respectful than that."

Vice stepped closer. "It's quite all right, Mrs. Chase. She's correct in that I'm to blame for the fall. I shall try to be more careful."

Mrs. Chase's expression instantly changed as she

gave Vice a wide smile. At least he'd won over one Chase woman. "I'm sure you will be."

Then the matron began to move, heading toward the aisle to follow the bride and groom from the church.

Tucking Ada's hand into his elbow, he bent down to whisper in her ear. "I pacified your mother."

Ada shook her head. "Perhaps. Though you don't understand the intensity with which my mother takes to matching her daughters. If I were you, I'd be concerned."

He paused, straightening. Well-placed move on her part. He wondered if she played chess. "Was that a threat?"

She arched one brow. "A warning. Take care with the attention you publicly give me."

That made the air whoosh from his lungs. "I've promised my friends to publicly watch over you. How can I take care?" Technically, he'd only stayed with her to make sure she stayed quiet about the gaming hell he secretly owned. She and her sisters had discovered his secret and by doing so had fallen into danger with a dangerous criminal, the Countess of Abernath.

She shrugged as they stepped into the aisle. "That is something you'll have to decide for yourself."

He let out a small growl of frustration. He'd been

about to claim that she owed him a boon. To collect, she'd have to allow him to escort her to the opening soiree of the season. That would be his chance to woo and watch her.

But she had a point, spending time with her was dangerous. First, for propriety's sake. But second, for his own sanity. When he picked women of the utmost success, he was confident, debonair. But Ada had thrown him off his game. For Christ's sake, he'd fallen out of a chair while sitting. And she had his thoughts bouncing from one extreme to the next.

Her hip brushed his and his own body clenched in awareness. What was it about this woman? By all accounts, he should have her easily in hand.

"Ada," Grace said from just behind them. Vice turned to see her looking rather comfortable on Bad's arm. "Do you think we might go shopping tomorrow? The Appletree ball is tomorrow evening and I've hardly any ribbon."

Vice's gut clenched. Ada and Grace had been safe because they'd made very few trips out. Six weeks prior, the Duke of Darlington's former fiancée, the Countess of Abernath, had attempted to expose their club by sending the unsuspecting Chase women to its door. When the ladies had kept the men's secret, Lady Abernath had begun attacking them one by one. If they went out shopping, they could be at risk. "No ribbons," he said before Ada could answer.

Ada turned to look at him. "You're sweet one second and a monster the next. Are you always so erratic?"

He shook his head. How had this day gone so terribly wrong? "You know that Lady Abernath attempted abductions of two of your cousins. Why would you be so foolish as to shop for ribbons?"

She sucked in a breath. "I didn't ask to shop for ribbons." Her cheeks turned that shade of pinkish brown that he was growing quite fond of. "Besides, I don't need your permission to do anything. My father can decide what shopping trips I take."

"Your father isn't aware of several key circumstances. I'm sure if he was, he wouldn't allow you to go shopping at all."

She raised her brows, stopping. "If he were aware of the circumstances, I'd be shopping for wedding attire."

She had him there and he knew it. If Lord Winthrop knew he'd been at an illicit late-night meeting with his daughter, Vice would find himself at the altar very quickly. For a wallflower, she was decidedly feisty. And he might enjoy that side of her if it didn't mean he was now being forced to go ribbon shopping. "My apologies. Perhaps Lord

Baderness and I could escort you but not tomorrow. Mayhap on Monday?"

Grace gave a little squeal behind them while Bad made a definite rumble of disapproval. But Ada's face softened and that's what he'd been hoping for all along. Perhaps it was just the challenge of the hunt. But when had he grown so sensitive to her happiness? "That would be very nice, actually. We've been trapped in the house for days."

"I look forward to it," he said, finding that he meant the words. He also had every intention of collecting an invitation to the Appletree ball. Hell, he might have one sitting in his stack of unopened correspondence. Somewhere over the course of this wedding, catching Ada's affection had become a personal goal. And he was a man who enjoyed a challenge. The question was, how would he work his way past her prickly exterior and her marriage-minded mother?

———

GRACE LINKED her arm into Ada's as they rode in the carriage back to Lord and Lady Winthrop's estate for the wedding breakfast. Her father sat across from them, staring out the window.

Grace leaned over, whispering in Ada's ear. "Are

you all right? You didn't seem yourself in the church?"

Ada shrugged. She was anything but all right. "It's Lord Viceroy. He's so..."

"Handsome?" Grace sighed. "That one next to me just scowls all the time, but not Lord Viceroy. He's lovely to look at."

Ada made a face. The sort that wrinkled her nose and scrunched her lips as though she'd smelled something terrible. "I was going to say something far more like irritating." Grace was better suited to his taste, she was certain. Ada had seen him once, in a tea shop with the most beautiful woman she'd ever laid eyes on. Absolute perfection. Not a freckle to be seen...

Grace laughed, covering her mouth with her hand, but Ada tapped her chin, continuing, "Also false. Most of what he does and says seems like a façade. As though he were an actor playing the part of a Viscount."

Grace shrugged. "He seems charming enough to me."

Ada shook her head. "Charming men do not hold interest in me for very long." Her stomach began to quiver. Her heart had been broken six months prior and she couldn't face the idea of that happening again. If any man were capable of the deed, it was

Lord Viceroy. She needed to stay away from him. "I'm not very exciting. Not like Diana or Minnie. Or you." They all knew how to flirt or argue, or insight some sort of passion. All she seemed able to do was sit quietly smiling.

Of course, one might argue that she did anything but that today. It was just that Lord Viceroy was so vexing. There had been that moment when she'd been on top of him when he hadn't been vexing at all. Then he'd been exciting. But he'd quickly slipped his veneer back in place.

She didn't like that man at all.

Grace patted her arm. "Don't be ridiculous. You're absolutely stunning and so kind. There is a man who is perfect for you and he will be handsome and smart."

Ada let out a sigh. Perhaps that was true. Then again, experience had told her it wasn't.

The only man who'd ever been truly interested in her had been a researcher of exotic wildlife. She'd known Walter Conroy for years as he was a family friend. And she'd been thrilled when he'd shown her favoritism over her cousins and sisters. So much so that she'd been happy to spend hours listening to his adventures. Until he'd left for one. Then, Walter had been clear. She was not to wait for him as he didn't know when or if he'd return. "Do you really think so?"

"Of course I do. Even Lord Viceroy is tempted by you."

Ada shook her head. He was only pretending out of habit or some other motivation. "It's an act. He's no more interested in me than he is in settling down and moving to the country."

"How do you know?" Grace asked, leaning even closer.

"I feel it." She pressed her hands to her cheeks. "He wants something from me. I'm just not certain what."

Grace covered a little giggle. "That's exactly my point. He wants something from you." Then Grace wiggled her eyebrows.

Ada swatted at Grace's arm. "Not like that." But she had to confess, when their bodies had pressed together, that was the only time he hadn't seemed fake. Ada had been terribly aware of him and something about the way his hands had held her made her almost think he'd noticed her too. He hadn't been trying to push her away, rather, he'd been drawing her closer.

"We shall see," Grace straightened. "The man did offer to escort you into the village."

"Did he now?" her father suddenly chimed in,

making her jump. Had he been listening this entire time? How much had she revealed out loud. "He's a friend of Darlington's, correct?"

"Yes, Papa," she answered, pressing her hands together in her lap.

"Do you think those men made a pact to marry? They seem rather smitten with you girls."

Her shoulders slumped with relief. Clearly he hadn't heard her saying that Vice was only pretending. "It's nothing like that, Papa. Darlington asked them to watch out for us, after Cordelia was taken from the house."

Her father shook his head. "Strange business. Has anyone caught Lady Abernath?"

"No," she answered. Her father didn't know that Darlington had been engaged to Lady Abernath and that she was threatening all of them now to expose their secret club. He also had no idea that Countess Abernath had also attempted to steal Diana. To tell them, they'd have to expose so many secrets they were attempting to keep hidden.

He nodded. "Well, Darlington's a good man to be taking your safety so seriously, but he needn't be worried. I am perfectly capable of watching after you girls. Furthermore, unmarried woman being with unattached lords that are not inclined toward marriage—"

"We understand, Uncle," Grace interrupted.

Ada's father turned back to the window. "I shall talk with Darlington myself."

"Good idea," Ada said. Perhaps her father could convince Lord Viceroy to leave her be. The man was causing a tension inside her that only his absence might relieve.

## CHAPTER THREE

VICE STEPPED from his carriage and then stood on the steps, waiting for Ada to arrive. He'd spent most of the ride contemplating what he might have done incorrectly. Clearly he'd upset her and he thought he knew why.

He'd come at her as though she were a seasoned woman who'd already had a lover. But Ada was a woman of little experience. She needed more wooing and less seduction. Just enough to make his guard job easy. A simple crush on her part would suffice. And it would be good for his ego too. He'd make sure to end things before Ada could reject him, of course. He wouldn't go through that again. But proving a woman like Ada could still care for him, well, that was tempting for certain.

His confidence restored, he considered how he'd

extricate himself when his guard duty was over. Being an innocent woman of marriageable age, he couldn't give her a gift or money to pacify her. Instead…he looked up at the sky, he'd have to weave a tale. Perhaps say that it was for her benefit.

Feeling secure, he watched as the carriage rolled up to the front of the house. Mr. Chase stepped out, handing out Ada and Grace.

Vice hardly noticed the fair blonde as Ada's auburn hair glinted in the sun. Her hips had a delightful sway that made his breath catch. He'd noticed her before, but now…how had he not seen how perfectly beautiful she was?

They walked toward him, his eyes drinking in every detail. The slim column of her neck, the lovely shape of her face, neither too thin nor too round, the slender cut of her shoulders. Ada delicately lifted the edge of her skirt as she began to ascend the stairs. They came abreast of him and he turned, holding out his elbow. "May I?"

Ada gave a quick shake of her head. "No need," she answered, breezing by.

"No need?" he replied. He stared after her, his jaw clenching so hard his teeth began to ache. How had she managed to deflate his sails in a matter of one single second? Just two tiny words? He fell in step behind her. "Are you certain?"

She looked back at him over her shoulder as her hand rested in her father's elbow. "No, thank you. As you can see, I am perfectly escorted."

Mr. Chase turned back as well. "I'll speak to Darlington but he needn't take up your time, my lord. I'll keep an eye on my daughter and I'm sure Lord Winthrop will watch out for his."

Vice closed his mouth. Darlington was definitely going to have to speak with both Lord Winthrop and Mr. Chase. The question was, how was Darlington going to impress the fact that their guard was most certainly needed without revealing all their secrets. "He'll be here any moment, I am sure."

Mr. Chase shook his head. "It can wait until after the wedding."

Grace gave a little bounce. "Uncle, will you take us to the village tomorrow to purchase ribbons? I need a particular shade of blue to match my dress."

"Of course." Mr. Chase gave his niece an indulgent smile. "I'm sure we're safe here in our London neighborhood."

Ada gave him another glance over his shoulder, but this time, she was nibbling her lip. She didn't mean to be enticing, but heaven above...he wanted to worry that flesh himself. Her words pulled him from his carnal thoughts. "I don't know, Papa. What happened with Cordelia…"

Vice stepped closer. "If you're going to go out, please allow me to accompany you. Just until you've talked with Darlington." He had a sudden fear he couldn't quite express. What if something happened to Ada? He'd feel responsible. He'd experienced…loss.

He hated the emotion. It was one he avoided at all costs after the death of his parents. He'd become the Viceroy at just thirteen when they'd succumbed to disease of the lung while he'd been away at school.

Mr. Chase stopped, looking at his daughter. She gave a single nod, small and almost imperceptible. But Vice saw it and the tension knotting his stomach relaxed. She was sensible enough to know that his help was necessary. "That would be jolly good of you," he said.

Ada glanced over her shoulder again, giving him another long look. This one did not hold irritation but…curiosity. Her eyes crinkled at the corners as she studied him. "Papa," she said. "I'll walk with Lord Viceroy for a moment."

Victory sang in his veins. What had he just done differently that she was responding to him? But before he could process, she slipped her hand into his elbow. "Thank you for being genuinely concerned," she said softly, turning her head so that she spoke into his shoulder.

Ah. She wanted genuine, did she? He drew in a deep breath. He didn't share his true feelings on anything very often. "You're welcome."

She flexed her fingers against the inside of his arm. "You needn't feign interest in me. I've no desire to be stolen away by Lady Abernath. I'll be careful."

He winced. "Who said I was feigning anything?" But the truth was, he had a rather practiced set of rehearsed lines. Had for quite a while now. To say anything else was to risk...

She rolled her eyes dropping her voice down low mimicking his much deeper voice. "Your hair is like the sunset." Ada gave him a pointed glare. "Please. Even I've heard that one."

Rubbing the back of his neck, he sighed. "So you don't appreciate my compliments?"

She paused for a moment as she once again nibbled on her lip. "I like compliments. I suppose I just like ones that are..." She paused and looked up, "About me."

He cleared his throat. Most women did not care that his flowery words were generic in nature. They assumed that the compliments were specifically about them and basked in the glow. "For the record, your hair *is* like the sunset."

She let out a huff. "I'm not even blonde."

Vice stopped, turning to her. "I see color." Then

he reached up and for just a moment, touched one of the strands. The silky texture slipped through his fingers. The gesture was wildly inappropriate but he couldn't seem to help himself. "And to clarify, I said your hair was the like the sunset, not the sun. Last summer, at the ocean, I sat in the sand as the sun set over the sea. The sky turned to a blaze of fiery colors. Then, just as the orb dipped down below the water, the colors softened to more muted shades of red, yellow, and orange. It was the most beautiful palate of color I'd ever seen and it only lasted for a few moments. That is the color of your hair."

What he didn't share was that the beach he'd sat on was on his family's estate. He hadn't been there since Camille had rejected his proposal. He'd taken her family there for a trip to the country in an attempt to woo her. He'd failed. The place was full of grief.

She stared at him, her mouth slightly open as that lovely color flushed her cheeks. It had tones of honey rather than a more classic pink but he found the shade so appealing. "I…you… that was…" She stopped trying to talk and just stared at him.

"Ada," he whispered. "You had a reason you wanted to speak with me?"

She swallowed and then, taking a deep breath,

straightened. "Yes, I did." She frowned. "I think I might need your help after all."

————

ADA WAS TRYING, and failing, to make her mind work properly. Vice had her all discombobulated. His compliment…it hadn't been generic at all and it had been stunningly beautiful, the sort of words that had robbed her of thought and filled her with breathless excitement.

"What do you need help with?" he asked. "Besides the obvious?"

"The obvious?" They had begun walking again and passed through the front door, but they were moving slowly, her father and Grace well ahead of them.

He quirked one eyebrow. "Lady Abernath? Her attempted kidnapping of two of your cousins? That sort of thing."

Heat was filling her cheeks. Again. Why did this man continually make her blush? And how did she regain the detachment she'd had in the church? When he gave her rehearsed lines, she could ignore how handsome he was. "Oh yes. That's exactly why I do need help. If not for me, then for Grace. She doesn't seem to understand how dangerous the situation is."

He stopped. "You're worried about her?" He looked at Grace's back as she disappeared into the breakfast salon. "Not yourself?"

Ada looked down at the floor. "I am naturally more cautious." She actually meant afraid. "But Grace seems to think that nothing bad will actually happen to her. If you are there, you can help me convince her to act with care."

He frowned at her, his brows drawing together. "I am here to protect you. Not her."

Well, that was both likely true and annoying and perhaps just a bit satisfying, but Ada didn't need help. Grace did. "Fine, I shall follow Grace around tirelessly and you…" She gave him what she hoped was an angelic smile.

He seemed to understand the point, his eyes narrowing. "You are going to lead me on a Grace goose chase."

His words made her smile but she tried to hold her lips in a straight line. She failed. "That's a pessimistic way of viewing the situation but yes, I suppose I am."

"Has everyone forgotten about me?" A deep, gravelly voice rumbled behind them. Without thinking, Ada tightened her hand on Vice's arm, moving closer. When had she begun to rely on him for protection?

In response, he leaned close to her ear. "It's only Bad." Ada had the distinct urge to lay her head on his chest as she wrapped her arms about his waist. She wasn't in danger but his embrace was so very…safe. And exciting.

She turned to see Vice's friend, the Baron of Baderness, scowling at them. "I am perfectly capable of keeping Grace safe and I've already been tasked with the job."

Ada cringed, her other hand slipping about Vice's arm. "I didn't mean to offend, my lord." She leaned against Vice, drawing comfort from his proximity. She never had liked when people were angry with her. "We don't know each other and I wasn't sure how committed to the task…" Her voice trailed off as she looked up to Vice. He stared down, his expression serious, his face drawn into taut lines. She cleared her throat. "Lord Viceroy offered my father help and I assumed that meant he was willing to help us."

He leaned closer, his other arm coming to her waist. "Of course, I am willing."

Excitement and warmth spread through her. When he was sincerely close, he was near irresistible. She had to figure out how to make the other

Vice return. The one who was arrogant and rakish. Because this man was irresistible. And Ada needed to resist him or end up falling under his spell.

Rake ruiner... The term was laughable. But ruined by a rake... She started with surprise and fear. Ada might be in real danger.

———

VICE ASSESSED Ada as she stared at him, her tongue wetting her lips. He wanted to taste that tongue. He drew her closer still. Would she taste of honey? Mayhap peaches. His body was hardening in the most sensitive places. Why was this woman wreaking havoc on him?

He hadn't reacted this way since...Camille. Strange. He'd collected all these women over the years, and they were all more, and somehow less than Ada. They were accomplished, intelligent, witty, rich. And yet, here stood a woman who wasn't nearly as successful and yet had seen straight through him with a single glance. And now she'd breached his defenses and had begun tearing them down in large chucks.

Camille had as well. Then, he'd welcomed her refreshing character. Camille had seen through him and when Vice had been with her, he'd been more for their relationship. For the first time since his parents' deaths, he'd shared his feelings with her. Allowed her to know how he hurt. What he was afraid of. Being alone...

But in the end, Camille found him to be less. Lacking. And when he'd proposed, she had rejected his offer. Instead, she'd married a marquess. She'd been sorry. Told him that she needed someone stronger, more stable. A man that was less scarred. He knew his parents' loss had stolen part of his heart but she'd made him realize he would never be enough. He knew then that a woman of real worth would never truly want him.

"Thank you," Ada said, her voice just above a whisper. "Thank you so much."

"What's happening out here?" Daring rumbled from the doorway. "Ada should be in here with the rest of us." The duke's eyes swept over Vice, his gaze lingering on the hand at Ada's waist.

Ada turned toward the duke, stepping in front of Vice as though he needed her protection. Her action almost made him smile. First, he wasn't scared of Daring. The duke wouldn't scare him even if they weren't friends. Second, she hadn't been lying when she said her sisters and cousins referred to her as timid. Bad's gravelly voice had nearly reduced her to shivers. Not that he minded. He quite liked when she'd stepped closer to him, looking for his protection. Her need sparked something deep inside him. "It was my fault, Your Grace. My father doesn't know about the danger we're in and he told Lord Viceroy that it would be best if he left our protection to family. I was just telling his lordship that Grace, in particular, has a penchant for trouble."

Daring frowned. "I see. Thank you, Ada." He gestured for Ada to step inside. Ada glanced back at him, her eyes holding a question as they crinkled at the corners.

He didn't want her to move away. Oddly, he wanted nothing more than to tuck her under his arm and keep her there. But he gave a tight nod of assent and she moved away, walking through the door to join her family.

Daring let her pass and then blocked the door again. "I'd like a word with both of you." Stepping past them, he started down the hall, not bothering to wait for their acceptance.

"Dukes," Bad rumbled. "So bossy."

Vice didn't reply. Instead, he looked back into the room where Ada had joined Grace, Diana, and Minnie. When had auburn become his very favorite color? "Daring," he called. "May I ask you a question?"

"I suppose," Daring answered.

"Do you find redheads to be more interesting?" Vice asked, not looking at Daring but rather, nothing in particular. His thoughts were on Ada's creamy skin and the green of her eyes and... He ran straight into the duke's back. He bounced off the man, catching himself before he fell. He was never clumsy. He braced himself against the wall. What was wrong with him?

Daring spun around, his face directly in Vice's. Vice was tall but Daring was taller and he bent down, using every inch of his height for intimidation. "Listen to me." He poked a finger into Vice's chest. "There are two ways this can happen. One, you do nothing but guard Ada. Two, you marry her." He poked again. "But you are not to dally with Minnie's sister." Daring's nose nearly touched his, nostrils flaring. "I will beat you, tar you, feather you, and then escort your mangled body directly to the altar. Am I clear?"

Vice drew in a deep breath, puffing out his chest. Daring was not going to scare him. "Abundantly." He braced his arms in front of him, pushing the duke back a bit. "I find Ada interesting as a person. She has a depth about her that is both intimidating and fascinating."

Daring took a partial step back. "And her waist? How do you find that?"

"It's a lovely waist," he answered, his eyes narrowing.

"I knew you thought that, since your hand's been touching it all day." Daring poked again.

Vice gave the man a small shove back. Daring was beginning to annoy him. "You're the one that said I needed to protect her. Now I feel the need to keep her close to me to make sure she is safe. I don't know how to be any other way."

Daring didn't poke him again. Instead, he took a step back. "That's true. It's difficult to remain detached. But if Mr. Chase is growing suspicious of you then you'd better proceed with caution." He scrubbed his hand down his face. "Perhaps the two of you should take turns caring for Grace and Ada. Keep you from forming an emotional bond and the Chases will be less suspicious."

Vice's chin snapped back as though he'd been slapped. Daring's suggestion irritated Vice. He didn't want Bad anywhere near Ada. Clenching his fists, he gave his head a stiff shake. He didn't want any man near her except for himself.

But before he could answer, Bad did. "I am perfectly capable of attending Grace without stepping into the marriage noose."

"What we need is a two-pronged plan." Vice scratched his chin. He needed to start using his head.

"We've been reacting to Lady Abernath. It's time to actively seek her out. In that way, we can cease guarding the women at all."

"I agree," Daring grunted. "I've hired a detective to find her. But I also think we need to talk with your cousin, Sin. He is more intimately acquainted with her movements than we are."

Vice's stomach pitched. He'd brought the Earl of Sinclair into the fold to help with the club but it had turned out that Lady Abernath had been black-mailing Sin into helping her. He knew it wasn't Sin's fault but Vice still felt betrayed by his cousin. Was he destined to have no one he could trust? "Fine. Should I get him now?" Sin was attending the wedding and the breakfast, though Vice hadn't spoken with the man all day.

Daring gave a nod. "Bad can get him. You and I have a bit more to discuss first."

Bad turned and headed down the hall the way they had just come. Vice didn't wish to retrieve Sin but he didn't really want to discuss anything else with Daring either. Truth be told, he'd like to return to Ada's side. This was an urge he needed to fight. Too much time with her and she'd discover all his worst attributes.

"We haven't discussed enough?" Vice asked.

Daring's shoulders drooped. "Ada is a soft

41

woman. I worried less about Diana or even Cordelia but Ada…she could be hurt so easily."

Vice cracked the knuckles of his fingers one at a time. "I understand that. But you needn't worry. She sees right through me and where I am concerned, she seems unwilling to yield at all."

Daring nodded. "I noticed." Then he clapped his hand on Vice's shoulder. "You bring out the best in her. Does she do the same for you?"

He blinked, taking a partial step back. "I don't know." She did, he suspected. What he was less certain about was whether he was actually good for her. He hadn't been for Camille.

Bad and Sin sauntered down the hall. "Good," Daring said as he caught Sin's eye. "It's time for us to finish this."

# CHAPTER FOUR

ADA STOOD between her sister and her cousin, wishing Vice had returned to the room. She shifted as she glanced at the door again. She tried to remind herself that she didn't much care for him. He was so full of himself.

But then she remembered the way his hand felt at her waist. The brush of his hip against hers. He made her feel like she was…more.

"Ada," Minnie nudged her arm. "Where are you?"

"Obviously, I am here." Ada pulled herself back to the present.

Minnie gave her a sideways glance, a small grin settling on her lips. "Physically, I suppose."

Ada looked over to where Diana stood next to her new husband. Lord Exmouth looked at his bride as though she were the most important person in the whole world. His gaze was so soft, his touch gentle. "You caught me. I watched Diana marry today and it made me wonder…"

"What did it make you wonder?" Minnie asked as she slipped her arm about her sister.

Ada gave a small shrug. "I wondered what type of man I might marry. Will he look at me with love and admiration?" Then she pointed to Diana.

Minnie gave her a squeeze. "Of course he will."

But Ada frowned. "How can you know? I'm not like you and Diana. People aren't drawn to me."

Minnie gave a light laugh. "You know people are also repelled by us, correct? Where everyone finds your company enjoyable."

"Enjoyable isn't exciting…" Ada looked toward the window, her chest aching. "It's quite boring. And interesting men find more interesting things to do than spend time with me."

Minnie let out a long breath. "Is this about Walter? First of all, he wasn't interesting, he was a terrible bore."

"Is that supposed to make me feel better? Even boring men won't like me enough to marry me?" Ada's gaze snapped back to Minnie.

Minnie held up her hands. "He liked you because you were willing to feed his complete affection for himself. You're unfailingly kind that way. And he didn't marry you because, despite what he said, he knew you'd wait. You're not boring, you're loyal and good."

Ada cringed. "I sound like our retriever, Rusty." But Minnie had made several pertinent points. She had made so few demands on Walter. But she'd always been afraid, if she did, he'd refuse and leave her. "I only know how to be myself."

Minnie stepped closer. "That's true. And some man will love you for exactly who you are. Don't let Walter take that away from you. He just wasn't the correct man." Minnie dipped her head even lower. "Now a man like Vice…"

"Vice is not an option." Ada took a small step back. "That makes it easier to tell him how I feel."

Minnie cocked her head to one side. "Is that why you can walk a straight line when you're with him? You don't think he likes you?"

Heat rose in her cheeks. "I might be able to walk but I literally fell on top of him during the ceremony. Besides, I've seen the women he prefers."

Minnie pressed her fingers to her cheeks. "He does generally spend time with women of far looser moral code."

"I meant they are more beautiful than me."

Minnie's eyebrows went up. "Ada. Please. I wish

to look like you. Where did you get the silly notion that you weren't stunning?"

Ada stared at her sister then. "But everyone notices you. No one sees me."

"That isn't true at all. They are trying to catch your attention, you keep your head down so they don't think they can approach you. I think you're afraid to talk to men because you become so clumsy."

Ada gave her head a shake but the words hit her like a slap. Did she keep people at bay? "That can't be." But the truth was, it was often easier to ignore them then to deal with her embarrassment. Since she'd been a small child, Ada had been awkward socially.

"Ada, if you want to catch a man's attention, you need only look at him." Her sister touched her arm. "I promise you he will eagerly approach."

Ada looked back at Diana. "And once I have his attention. How do I keep it?" She thought back to Walter.

"Well." Minnie nibbled her lip. "That is when you should make yourself less available. Don't be afraid to make him wait. Or interrupt him when he talks of himself. Once you have his attention, make him work for you."

"Interesting," she answered. She had been near

rude to Vice, he didn't seem less interested at all. In fact, he had grown more so. "I shall think on that for certain."

"Good," Minnie answered.

Ada clasped her hands. In fact, she may test out a few theories this very day. And she knew just the man on whom to try them.

———

VICE SAT NEXT TO SIN, leaning away from the man. Sin had been his favorite cousin and one of his closest friends. His circle was growing smaller by the day.

Sin gave him several short glances. Finally, he leaned over. "You're angry with me."

Vice backed away. "Not angry. I don't blame you for wanting your daughter back." But he was disappointed. Vice couldn't deny that. He felt...betrayed.

Sin grimaced. "Abernath had taken my daughter. What length would you go to get back someone you loved?"

For some odd reason, Ada's delicate features rose up in his thoughts. "I understand, Sin. I do." Surprisingly, he did. If someone took Ada...when had he gotten so bloody protective?

"Sin, we all understand. That's why you're still here," Daring added.

"Agreed," Bad said. "And now that we have your daughter back, we need your help."

"Anything." Sin spread his hands out on the desk in front of him.

Daring leaned forward. "How were you acquainted with Lady Abernath?"

Sin shrugged. "Socially. I've begun looking for a new wife to help me raise Anne." He pulled his hands back into his lap. "I met her a month ago and she confided in me that her husband had passed. She told me that she needed help financially, which was why she hadn't made his death public. She didn't want to leave society in order to grieve." He clenched his hands. "It made sense at the time. Looking back, I see how foolish it was."

Vice cleared his throat. "She's a very persuasive woman." This time, he moved in closer. "Were you intimate?"

Sin shook his head. "No. I mean, we were moving in that direction but I wanted to woo her, not seduce her. I thought…" He raked his hand through his hair. "I thought she'd make a good stepmother. What a bloody fool I am."

"She has fooled more than one person," Daring replied. "Many of us have fallen prey to her charms."

Sin nodded. "What do you need help with?"

"Where does she go? What does she do with her time?" Bad asked. "We need to catch her before she tries to take another person who is dear to us."

Sin looked down at his lap. "I don't have any idea where she's living now, but I do know a few clubs she likes to frequent. I could take you there but only if you can help me keep Anna safe."

Daring nodded. "Of course. In fact, why don't you both stay with me and Minnie? I can't think of anywhere safer than that. I can have Minnie's cousin come stay too. Mary is wonderful with children."

Sin slumped back, relief making him look limp. "That would be wonderful."

Vice let out a breath. His plan was falling into place. "We'll start tonight. In the meantime, let's return to Exile's wedding. We can't miss the entire breakfast."

Daring rose. "Agreed. And you two are to keep your eyes on Ada and Grace and your hands off of them."

Bad grunted, but Vice didn't reply. His entire plan was to capture Ada's attention. Not that Ada was cooperating. But if she did, if his plan succeeded and she became enamored with him, would he defy Daring?

He wouldn't ruin her. He hadn't thought about it

before but now, he'd never compromise her future. Perhaps, with that in mind, it would be best to abandon the idea entirely that he capture her affection.

With that in mind, he made his way back down to breakfast. The moment he walked into the room, he sought out Ada, finding her next to Minnie. Her eyes met his, then quickly looked away. He stopped, unable to look away.

When her eyes found his again, it was as though she were drawing him forward, and he found himself crossing the room toward her.

"What did I miss?" he asked as he reached her side.

"Not a thing." She glanced over at Diana and Exile. "They seem very happy, don't they?"

He didn't take his eyes off her. He couldn't. "They do."

"I'd like to have that someday. What they have. The way they look at one another." Then she looked at him again, those green eyes sparkling in the morning light.

He couldn't help himself. "You will."

Her gaze widened and her lips parted. "You think some man will feel for me the way Lord Exmouth feels about my cousin?"

He wanted to lift her fingers to his lips. Hell, he

wished he could kiss her. "I know a man will. In fact, I'd be willing to wager there will be more than one."

Her eyebrows shot up. "Really? Are you more or less likely to wager running a gaming hell as you do?"

He stepped closer. "I almost never gamble. The odds always favor the house." He wanted to stroke her cheek, run his thumb along her jaw.

She let out a soft sigh and her breath tickled his nose. Honey. That's what she'd taste like.

"Minnie says that I should meet a man's eye and then, when he approaches, talk about myself rather than asking about him. Do you think that's true?"

He started. "That's what you just did to me, isn't it?"

She gave a tentative nod. "Did it work? Are you more or less interested in me? Not that you need be interested at all. I know I am not much…I—"

"Ada," he said, wishing he could touch her. How could she say she wasn't much? She was working her way into his soul. He reached up his fingers but dropped them again. Daring burned holes in his back with the intensity of his gaze. "You are dangerously close to ruining another rake."

# CHAPTER FIVE

ADA'S MOUTH fell open at his words. What did his confession mean precisely? How would she ruin him? She peeked over his shoulder, lifting up in tiptoe, to see Darlington glaring at them. "I think you mean that Daring is close to ruining a rake. He's not going to allow you a single slip-up, but that isn't me."

He laughed. A lovely deep baritone that rippled over her skin like tiny waves on the surface of water. She shivered as the sound washed over her. "He is giving us a rather intent assessment."

She nodded, peeking at him again. "Perhaps you should go speak with someone else. Then His Grace could relax."

Vice stepped closer. "Where is the fun in that?"

She pressed her lips together to keep from grinning. Ada had known he was the sort that liked trouble. She was interesting to him precisely because she currently represented a whole parcel of issues. A villain who might attack at any moment, a family who might assume the worst, a surly duke who may force Vice down the aisle at the end of a pistol. She frowned. He'd lose interest quickly enough when the danger was gone. Wouldn't he? She had to confess, part of her was tempted to throw caution to the wind. Which would be a mistake, wouldn't it? "Emily has just arrived. I should go talk with her."

"Is Jack here?" Vice turned to look toward the door.

"I don't think so. Emily left him and moved back into my aunt and uncle's house. I hope she and Jack reconcile soon," she paused, nibbling on her lip. Emily and Jack's early days had been rather tumultuous. Jack had a colorful past and he'd attempted to keep many parts secret from Emily. Most recently, they'd discovered that Lady Abernath's son could be Jack's child. Emily had not taken the news well.

"As do I," he answered.

She made a little noise of dissent in the back of her throat. "You can't tell me you're glad Jack is married."

Vice shrugged. "I wasn't at first. But Emily is with

child and even I can see that Jack loves her with all his heart. I want whatever makes him happy."

Ada swallowed a lump. With every minute that passed, she liked this man more. Which was dangerous for her own happiness. "If you'll excuse me."

With a final nod, she stepped around Vice and started for Emily, whose face looked decidedly pale. "Em," she called, reaching for her cousin's hand. "Are you all right?"

Emily shook her head. "I've been terribly sick in the mornings. Do you think Diana will forgive me for missing the ceremony? I just couldn't leave the house."

Ada embraced her cousin. "Of course she will." She moved back, lightly stroking Emily's cheek. "It's you I'm worried about. You don't look well at all."

Emily shook her head. "I've had trouble keeping food down. I can't sleep thinking about..." She shook her head. "Ada. It's not too late for you. You can marry a nice man with no secrets and no sordid past."

Ada took a partial step back. Had Emily been reading her journal? "Are you saying that because those are the only men who'd be interested in me?"

Emily squinted her eyes. "No, of course not. I'm

54

saying to stay away from rakes and rogues because they will break your heart. Just like Jack has mine."

Ada bit her lip, her insides clenching. Emily was not herself but her words touched some of Ada's deepest fears. "I think I should come stay with you and Grace. I'm worried about both of you."

Emily reached for her hands again. "Oh, please do, Ada. I have been so out of sorts. You're always so soothing. You're like spring sunshine after a long, cold winter."

"Hmm."

She heard a deep male voice behind her. Vice.

"That is an interesting metaphor," he said.

Emily straightened, taking a step back and pulling Ada with her. "Vice. Nice to see you again." Her voice held a chilly edge that belied her words.

"And you as well, Lady Effington." He stepped closer still. "How do you fare?"

Emily wrapped an arm about Ada. "Why do you care?"

Ada stared at Vice, whose gaze travelled back and forth between her and Emily. "Jack is my friend and Ada is my responsibil—"

"She is Miss Chase to you," Emily hissed, then pointed her finger. "I know all about you and your antics. I've heard about the actresses, the gypsies, the parties with princesses. I know the sort you are." Emily's voice was rising as the crowd quieted.

Ada's stomach flipped and her breath refused to release. "Emily. You're making a scene." But inside, an ache formed in her chest. The words were the reminder she'd needed to keep her distance from Lord Viceroy. She was the woman from whom normal men ran in fear. She'd never keep Vice's attention for long.

Emily drew in a long breath. "Stay away from my cousin. She doesn't need your kind."

Vice's head snapped back as though he'd been struck. "My apologies if I've offended."

"My lord," Ada started, taking a half step toward him before Emily pulled her back.

Vice didn't answer as he turned and left again. This time, he didn't just cross the room, he walked around them and headed for the door.

"You frightened him away," Ada said as she watched his back. While she knew it was for the best that she not allow him close, she didn't like seeing him hurt either.

"Good," Emily answered. "You'll be far happier without him pestering you. Who does he think he is using your given name?"

Ada shook her head. Emily was right. And yet, somehow, she hated to see him go.

---

VICE CLIMBED INTO HIS CARRIAGE, tossing himself with a thud onto the bench. What irritated him so bloody much was Emily had been exactly right. He would never be good for a woman like Ada.

Hadn't Camille taught him that already? He still remembered the words she'd tossed at him like balls of lead. "I need a man who will be stable, reliable. You're very fun, Lord Viceroy but I can't imagine raising children with you. You'd be at the club far more than you'd ever be home."

He dropped his head into his hands. He'd sworn to give it all up but Camille hadn't believed him. In the end, she'd married exactly the sort she'd described. Vice wondered if she was happy. Likely she was.

He rapped on the carriage frame signaling for his driver to start. The whip cracked as the reigns jingled and he leaned back into his seat.

"Wait," a small feminine voice called. "Lord Viceroy, please wait."

Ada. He'd recognize her voice anywhere.

"Stop," he barked, hitting the wall with his walking stick again. The carriage drew to a halt and the door snapped open. Ada stood on the ground, in nothing but her pale green gown, her exposed skin covered in goose pimples. While the spring sun warmed the air, today was decidedly cool with a stiff breeze. "You're shivering."

"I'll only be a moment," she replied. "I just wanted to tell you…" And then she stopped, nibbling on her lip.

He climbed out of the carriage again, and removing his coat, dropped it over her shoulders, pulling it closed about her chest.

Her arms wrapped it tighter about her from the inside and then she dropped her head, drawing in air through her nose. "Your coat smells delightful."

He wanted to hold her close but he glanced up to the windows to see a crowd watching them from above. "I'm glad you like it."

Ada lifted her head, her bright green eyes meeting his. "It smells of cigars, and pine and…you."

He gripped the outside of his thigh to keep from touching her face. "You like the way I smell?"

She looked away again. "Tomorrow night, there is the Applebee ball we're to attend. I think I mentioned it earlier. It's Grace's and my season to come out." She drew in a breath. "His Grace will be there along with Lord Exmouth and Lord Effington, you needn't attend."

"You came out here to tell me not to attend?" He

squinted his eyes, dropping his head closer. Why did those words feel like a stab in the heart?

She shrugged, the large shoulders of his coat exaggerating the movement. "My words didn't come out properly." She looked at him again, her chin tipping up, exposing the long column of her neck. He'd like to trail kisses down that neck. "I came out here to ask you to come, despite my family's words. But if you don't wish to, I would understand and I'll be safe, even if you don't."

He shouldn't go. This was his chance to leave before Ada came to her senses and rejected him. Besides, she wasn't even his sort of woman. "I'll be there," he answered.

She gave a quick nod, a tiny smile playing about her lips. It highlighted the soft kissable curve of them. The lovely shape of her cheek, the sweep of her chin. "Thank you," she murmured, not looking away. "I appreciate your help."

"It's my pleasure," he said. That was the truth. Emily had been right on several fronts and one of them was that Ada brightened his life. "I shall meet you outside the front doors."

"I look forward to it," she answered with a smile.

"Let me escort you back inside. I can't bear to see you out here without your coat. There is a stiff breeze today."

"Thank you," she said as she turned to walk toward the door. He knew her entire family watched but he didn't want to offer her his arm. She'd have to pull out her hand. Instead, he wrapped a hand about her waist.

She looked at him and then up at the windows.

His only answer was to keep pushing her forward. "Your family is an issue for another day. Today and tomorrow, we make sure to keep you safe. Do you think you will shop for ribbons in the morning?"

She shook her head. "I'll convince Grace to postpone. We'll wear white tomorrow, she's got ribbon enough for that."

He helped her back up the steps. Her small waist fit his hand so perfectly. Perhaps he should just marry her before she realized that he wasn't good enough. He saw Emily in the window. Had that been Jack's plan too?

Reaching the door, they stepped inside. "I'll see you tomorrow, Ada."

"Lord Viceroy." She gave small curtsey.

"Ada," he whispered, slipping his hands under the lapels of his coat to slowly push the fabric off her frame. He grazed her narrow shoulders and heard her gasp. The sound made him clench. "When we're in private, call me Blake."

"Blake," she answered, looking up at him once again.

Damn, he loved looking down at her like this. And he'd been wrong. Ada was more special than any woman that had come before her. She'd slipped past all his defenses, making him ache with need for her. How had he ever thought another woman was more beautiful?

Gently removing the coat, he took a step back. "Tomorrow."

"Tomorrow," she said.

That gave him exactly one day to decide what he was going to do. Marry the girl and risk being as miserable as Jack or watch another woman of true merit walk away. He surely didn't know which he'd choose.

But for tonight, he'd set the question aside. He had a villain to catch, after all, and then he'd have all the time in the world to explore his feelings.

## CHAPTER SIX

ADA WATCHED HIM WALK AWAY, bunching her hand in her skirts so that she'd not embarrass herself by reaching out to him. How had she started the day, thinking Vice a vapid ne'er do well and before afternoon repose, found herself yearning for the same man?

She shook her head. She'd yearned for him before now, she'd just talked herself out of her feelings before today. The first time she'd seen him with the actress, her breath had caught in her lungs, her head had swum. But one look at the woman he'd been with and she'd known. He would never be hers. She'd pushed her feelings down and had made sensible choices.

Like Walter. He'd been what she thought was the

more practical choice. If even the practical men didn't want her…what did that say about her?

Or was Minnie right and she needed to ask for more?

And Vice. She knew the sort of woman he preferred. Beautiful, talented, and vivacious were just a few of the words that described the women he'd been linked to. None of those words described her. She was pretty, dependable, a bit shy and scared, and very awkward.

"Ada?" Emily asked, coming up next to her. "Why are you staring at the front door?"

"No reason," she answered.

Emily touched her sleeve. "I hope you're not upset with me. I pushed Lord Viceroy away because I wanted to protect you."

Ada sighed. She wished Vice was still here, but she knew Emily told the truth. She also knew her cousin was hurting from her recent fight with her husband. "How could I ever be upset with you?" She turned to hug Emily. "Let's take you down to the kitchen and see if we can't find something to calm your stomach."

"I'd like that," Emily murmured. "After missing the ceremony I'd better help Diana settle into her new home this afternoon." Emily pinched her nose. "I've been a terrible sister of late."

Ada patted Emily's hand. "You've had your own issues. Everyone understands."

"You are a gem," Emily said as they made their way down the stairs. "Come with me to Diana's, would you? She'll be kinder with you there."

"Of course," she answered. Part of her wished to stay home, if only to relive every detail of today, but another part knew her family needed her and she'd do better to keep busy anyhow. "Breakfast is drawing to a close. We'll get something in your stomach and then we'll go to Diana's new home."

Emily nodded. "We shan't stay long. I'm sure they're eager to be alone. But I still think it will help Diana to settle in. It's scary to leave the family you've lived with your entire life."

That made Ada pause. Emily never seemed frightened of anything. "You were nervous about leaving?"

"Of course," Emily said as they reached the kitchen. "Excited too, of course."

Emily crossed to the counter, finding some bread half cut on a board. "Oh, this looks delicious."

"Day-old bread?" Ada cocked a brow.

"She's been terribly sick," Diana called from the doorway. "I'm glad to see you eating, Emily, and I'm glad to see you down here with her and not still outside with Lord Viceroy."

Ada pressed her lips together. "I was only outside for a minute. I needed to convey a message before he left."

"Did I hear you say you were both coming with me to my new home?"

"Just for a bit," Ada answered.

Diana gave a nod. "Good. We'll have plenty of time to discuss why you're not acting like yourself. I never thought I'd see you chase down a man like that."

Ada wrinkled her nose. "I didn't chase him down. And we're not talking about me. Today is about you. Remember?"

Diana stopped giving her a sidelong glance. "If anyone else had just said that, I would think they were deflecting. You're one of the few people who might actually mean those words."

"I do," she sniffed. "Now. Tell us. How does it feel to be Lady Exmouth?"

Diana gave her a glowing smile as Emily looked down at her piece of bread.

Ada spent the day tending her cousins, Emily and Diana, as they helped Diana unpack her belongings in Exile's townhouse. The couple had decided not to have a honeymoon but they would take a few days to themselves in place of a trip to meet family. Once everything had been settled with Lady Abernath, they'd travel to Scotland to meet all of Exmouth's relatives.

Climbing in the carriage to return home, Ada watched the London streets slip by, lanterns being lit as the sun began to set. Emily was equally quiet next to her, clearly lost in her own thoughts.

The sky was aglow with an orange-red hue that left her breathless. And it made her think of Vice.

She smiled as the final rays of light slipped from the sky. The carriage slowed, reaching a busy inter-section and Ada scanned the crowd of people on horseback, in carriages, and on foot. The city was always busy but this time of year a flood of people returned from the countryside for the upcoming season.

Pale blonde hair caught her notice. It was distinc-tive in its shade and she recognized the color imme-diately as belonging to Lady Abernath.

Pulling the curtain tighter to conceal her face, she took note of the neighborhood first. She was near Hyde Park on Cromwell Road.

Her eyes narrowed. "I can't believe it."

"What?" Emily said, sitting up a bit. "Is something wrong?"

"It's Lady Abernath." She pointed out the window, holding the curtain tight.

Emily partially stood, shifting to the other bench.

"She looks awful," Emily hissed, pressing her face to the glass.

"What do you mean?" Ada studied the woman slowly making her way through the crowd. To her eye the woman looked exactly the same. Tall, statuesque, almost cold in her perfect beauty. The man with whom she walked, however, gave Ada the chills. He was well over six feet, standing out in the crowd, with hard eyes and dark slicked back hair. His mouth was thin and set in a frown while several scars crisscrossed his face.

"Look at her cloak. She bought it ready-made, I'm certain," Emily murmured. "Not that there's anything wrong with that, it's just that her wardrobe is usually impeccable."

"She lost most of her clothes in the fire, I'm sure." Ada answered, her eyes still studying the man as she hunched lower in her seat.

Lady Abernath had stolen Cordelia. When Malice had rescued her, a fire had broken out in Lady Abernath's home. Malice himself had rescued Abernath's son and Malice and Cordelia had adopted the boy, taking Harry with them to visit with family. "Do you find it odd that Lady Abernath hasn't even attempted to get her child back?"

"She didn't tell anyone she even had a child. Everything about the situation is odd," Emily answered. "But she has even more reason to hate us now that we have her son." The child had been so clearly mistreated and left in a burning house, they hadn't had much choice.

"But why not go to the Bow Street Runners? She could accuse Malice of kidnapping."

Emily tapped her chin. "That does seem like an obvious method of revenge."

"Perhaps it doesn't affect Daring directly enough?" Abernath and Daring had been engaged. He was the man the countess most wanted to punish.

"Or perhaps she doesn't want the child." Emily suddenly dropped the curtain. "I think she saw me."

Ada dropped hers too. "We'd better get out of here."

"The crowd is too thick." Emily clasped her hands. "We should have brought one of the men with us."

"Why didn't we?" Ada leaned forward, wishing Vice was here now.

Emily shook her head. "It was just a carriage ride. We shouldn't even have been seen."

"What do we do?" Ada was never the best in these situations.

"We need to get home." She thumped on the carriage wall. "Driver. Let's find another way."

"Yes, my lady," he called back and then snapped the reins, moving through the crowd to turn left on one of the many side streets.

With the carriage moving, Ada could breathe again. "Lady Abernath is winning on one front. She's struck fear in our hearts."

Emily shook her head. "You're right. I hope they catch her soon. This is getting tiresome."

The situation was worse than tiresome. Her time with Vice was forcing her to face some hard truths. She had feelings for Lord Viceroy, ones he would never return. She had to figure out how to close herself off again.

———

VICE STOOD in a dimly lit club, the hour well past midnight. The place reeked of stale liquor and unwashed bodies. His nose curled up and he pulled out his pocket square, then placed the fabric over his nose. He pinched the fabric tighter to his nostrils. When had he gotten squeamish?

This was the third establishment he, Sin, and Bad visited this evening, each one worse than the last. Had the women always been so garish? The liquor so vile?

He wondered how he'd feel in their club, the Den

of Sins. It had always been a second home to him, but something had shifted, where he wished to just be at home. A red-haired woman approached him. Not the auburn shade of Ada's hair but a bright red. She flashed him a large smile, her hips swaying back and forth in a manner meant to attract attention. "Aren't you a pretty one." She smiled, sliding her hand along his shoulder. She didn't smell like cinnamon or honey, rather like cheap rose water and unwashed body.

He kept his face passive, not moving a muscle as he fished into his pocket and drew out a coin. "For you," he said. "Go take fifteen minutes for yourself."

She pressed closer. "You don't want to join me?"

"I must decline," he answered.

Bad narrowed his gaze, his heavy brow dropping low. "Did you just pass up a perfectly good woman?"

Vice had his doubts about perfectly good, but fortunately for him, Daring entered the room and waved from the door, his fist clenched around a piece of paper. Then the man stalked across the room, the crowd seeming to part for him. "We're leaving," he said by way of introduction.

Sin stepped forward. "Why?" He swept his hand across the club. "She mentioned coming here several times."

Daring leaned in closer. "Ada and Emily saw the

countess today when they were out in their carriage."

"Ada was out without me?" Vice straightened his gut dropping in fear. "Is she all right?"

"Fine." Daring gave him a curious stare. "But she saw Abernath with a man. Emily described him in her letter," he paused and waved the piece of paper, "as tall, long dark hair, and several scars on his face."

Vice sucked in his breath. "She was with Crusher."

Daring gave a nod. "I can't believe she'd stoop that low. Even among thieves the man has no honor."

"Are we going to Crusher's place?" Bad asked. "If she's under his protection, it will be difficult to take any action there."

Daring shook his head. "I thought we'd wait outside for her to exit. See if we can't intercept her?"

"It's as good a plan as any," Vice answered. Part of him was relieved. If they caught her, life could return to normal. But another voice wondered what that life held exactly? Did he even want that anymore?

But he pushed these thoughts aside as he followed Daring out the door. They climbed into Daring's carriage but it was Bad who spoke first. "Rather than just wait outside, I'll go in," he said.

"Crusher and I have a history. I can visit without arousing suspicion."

Daring looked over at Bad. "Dare I ask what that history is?"

Bad shrugged. "I wasn't always a lord like you." He sat back. "We'll use that to our advantage tonight."

Vice winced. "I'll come in with you. Perhaps we should pretend to be drunk? Join in as patrons?"

Bad gave him a long look. "How did you become so delightfully good at subterfuge?"

Inwardly Vice cringed. He wished he was a bit more wholesome. Having inherited at such a young age had enabled him to be wild as a young man. But he'd lost a great deal of his innocence too. "It comes naturally."

Bad clapped him on the back. "We're nearly there."

Ten minutes later, they walked through the door, Vice swaying on his feet in what he hoped was a convincing manner.

A quick survey of the room, however, left him disappointed. There was no sign of Crusher or Abernath.

Bad found them a seat at one of the tables, and they made a point to lose several hands to the house.

Only then, did Bad, in a slurred voice, ask to see the owner. "I want Crusher," he demanded.

"Who are ye to demand him?" The dealer spit on the floor.

"We're old friends," Bad swayed in his chair. "Tell him Baderness wants to see him."

"Baderness?" The man spit again but got up from his chair. "I'll get him but yer gointa regret it."

Bad gave the other man a bleary-eyed stare but Vice clenched his fists under the table. "What's your plan?"

Bad shook his head. "Get invited to the back room."

Vice drew in a deep breath. He didn't like it. They'd be trapped and with only two of them, it was more difficult to fight their way out but they were in it now. He wouldn't leave Bad to face whatever was coming alone.

The dealer returned, waving them to follow. Vice stood, holding his breath. What were they about to find out?

Much like the Den of Sins, they made their way down a long dimly lit hall until a doorway led to a small back room. Vice had never been introduced to Crusher but he recognized the man immediately. A large scar ran from his eye to his lip with several more cutting at various angles on his face. "Did that to himself," Bad muttered so only Vice could hear.

The only question Vice wanted to ask was why. But he stayed silent as Crusher motioned for them to sit. "It's been a long time, my lord." Crusher drew out the address, dropping his voice low. "To what do I owe this pleasure?"

Bad took the seat, leaning back in his chair as though he didn't have a care in the world. Vice had never pegged his friend for an actor but he was putting on a show now. "Viceroy and I were just looking for some entertainment. Life has been a bit dull."

Crusher's eyes flitted to Vice. "And you came here? I'm surprised you'd stoop so low. Even back in the old days you were too high and mighty for the likes of me."

Bad didn't move a muscle. "That isn't true. You were damned intimidating."

"Liar," Crusher sneered. "You were never intimidated and the only man that ever bested me."

Bested him in what? Vice didn't dare ask now. Instead he addressed Crusher. "Perhaps we've come to the wrong place," he said, shifting in his chair. "Apologies for taking up your time."

"Sit." Crusher put on a smile that only pulled at his scars. "I didn't say that I wanted you to leave. Just that I was surprised you'd come. What sort of entertainment did you have in mind?"

Bad cocked his head to the side. "Have any women of quality?"

Crusher's lip curled over his teeth as though the conversation pained him. His fingers clenched and unclenched. "The normal fair. But you're welcome to have a look."

Something wasn't sitting right. Crusher sounded affable but he wasn't nearly the actor Bad was and his face twisted into angry lines. Or perhaps that was just his scars. "No thanks. If you had something special, you would have said so." This time Vice did stand. If something was going to happen, he wanted to be able to reach the door.

Crusher stood as well. "I said sit."

Vice cocked his head to the side. "And I said, no thank you."

The dealer still stood behind Crusher and he came to man's side. "My employer has asked ye nice like to have a seat for some gentlemanly conversation."

Bad stood too. "I don't think anyone is sitting." Bad expanded his chest. "Why are you trying to keep us here?"

Crusher pointed a beefy finger at Bad. "Just because you bested me back then, doesn't mean you can now." He jabbed his finger toward Bad. "I know why you're here. She's mine now and you can't have her."

Bad paused. "Are we discussing Countess Abernath?"

"We are." Crusher reached over and gave Bad a small push. "Let's not play games. Life has given you everything hasn't it? But not her. She's for me."

Vice grimaced. Jealousy was a dangerous mistress. "We don't want the countess like that. We just need a word."

"I know what you need. You can't have it." Then he sneered at Bad. "Outsmarted you this time. She's long gone by now."

Crusher had brought them back here to distract them. The countess had likely slipped away. But at least they knew who she was now associated with. "You've mistaken our intent entirely." Vice held up his hands. "We were only concerned for her after the fire. She has a history with our friend—"

"I know about her history," Crusher sneered. "And your friend is going to pay. If you've helped him to hurt her, you're all going to pay." Then he reached over and shoved Bad in the chest.

Crusher was a large man but Bad planted his feet in a way that kept him from moving. He absorbed the push. "We'll see who pays."

Those words might as well have been a powder keg. The room exploded as the Crusher dove at Bad, the dealer making a lunge for Vice.

Ducking around the table, the man missed, and went crashing into the wall.

Crusher had Bad on the floor, his beefy fist raised. Vice grabbed a chair and brought it crashing down on the man's back. He slumped to the side and in an instant, Bad was up.

Racing to the door, they made their way out of the club, stumbling into the street. Vice didn't stop, heading to the alley where they'd left Daring but the carriage was gone. "Do you think they're chasing Abernath?"

Bad shook his head. "I don't know but let's get out of here while we can. We'll find out tomorrow."

Vice grimaced as they started running down the street, zigzagging through alleys. One thing was for certain, they hadn't solved anything yet. He could only hope they hadn't made the situation worse.

They'd head for Daring's and find out what happened. Most likely, Daring was chasing Abernath now. He hoped they caught her. Not that he intended to leave Ada alone. He liked it best when she was by his side, but he still couldn't shake the feeling that she could do much better than him.

# CHAPTER SEVEN

THE NEXT DAY passed in a flurry of activity. Ada kept her promise and went to stay with Emily and Grace. The girls had always passed freely between the family homes and her parents thought little of her going to stay at her aunt and uncle's house.

Which was a relief. As she'd been packing to go, her mother had had a great many questions about the Viscount who'd been so attentive.

"When did you meet him, dear?" It was an innocent enough question but the answer was anything but.

As she could not say, *at their secret club in the middle of the night,* she'd nibbled her lips. "Jack and Emily introduced us."

Her mother had grinned approvingly. "And has he asked to court you yet?"

"Mother," she'd pleaded. "We've only met a few times."

"Is he attending the ball tonight?" Her mother leaned forward from her perch on the bed.

"Yes," she answered, straightening from the trunk she was filling. "But mother, don't get your hopes up. Lord Viceroy is a known bachelor."

Her mother winked. "So was your father, dear. And you," her mother pointed at her daughter, "are just the sort to change a man's mind."

She put her hands on her hips. "Oh please. Diana or Minnie, they are the types who might—"

"Ada Lynn," her mother said as she stood from the bed. "They might take a man and shake some sense into him, but you will slowly lead him down the correct path. He won't even realize it's happening until it's too late."

Ada hadn't known how to respond to that and she still didn't. In her experience she hadn't led anyone anywhere. Well, she'd managed to get Blake to agree to come to a ball. That was about the extent of her abilities.

But the words had echoed in her head as she'd gone to her aunt and uncle's home. They'd stayed with her as she'd eaten a light meal and then gotten ready for the evening's festivities.

Emily lay on her bed in her room as Grace and

Ada dressed but her eyes remained unfocused as she stared out the window.

"Em," Ada tentatively asked, her white gloves being buttoned up her arm. "Why don't you come with us?"

"I'm pregnant. I shouldn't."

"You're only a few months along. No one will know," Grace added, patting her carefully coiffed curls.

Emily shrugged. "He'll be there because Darlington wants him to be."

"Exactly," Ada answered, crossing the room to carefully sit next to her cousin. "You two should talk."

Emily shook her head. "I don't want to talk and I don't want to see him. He's lied to me too many times about his past. He'll only convince me to come back and then we'll do this entire thing again where I discover another falsehood."

Ada tapped her chin, her heart aching in sympathy. "Then don't do it again. Make him tell you any other secrets. Be honest. One more lie will break the two of you forever." She reached for Emily's hand. "But he loves you. I know he does and you're carrying his child. Do you honestly see yourself raising this baby without him?"

"No," Emily answered letting out a heavy sigh.

"But I also need to teach him a lesson. I can't forgive him too quickly, like I did the last time."

A little giggle escaped from Ada's lips, and she clapped her hand to her mouth. Emily's plan was quite smart. "I see. This is medicine."

Emily looked at her, a smile tugging at her lips. "What I didn't quite realize is that I'd be miserable too." Then she sighed again. "I was awful to Lord Viceroy today, wasn't I?"

Ada patted her cousin's hand. "I'm sure he's fine."

"Do you like him?" Emily asked and Grace stopped fussing with her hair to cross the room and listen to her answer.

"Me? Like a rake? I'm a scared little mouse remember?" Ada stood, shaking out her skirts.

Emily started to rise too. "You are more cautious. But men like that often times. My advice, allow him to protect you. It will make him feel manly."

Ada shook her head. Her mother's advice hadn't been dissimilar. But how did that explain Walter's rejection or the scores of men who'd passed her by? "I'm not the sort of woman that men like him are interested—"

"He's interested," Grace dismissed her claim. "And you are doing a marvelous job of pushing him away and then drawing him back in. I sincerely thought you were doing it on purpose."

Ada blinked as Emily crossed the room. "I am going to go. It won't take me long. Wait for me."

Grace returned to the mirror. "She's going to take forever and we'll be late."

Ada had no choice but to pace to the window. "But Lord Viceroy is supposed to meet me at the doors. He'll be outside."

"Good," Grace answered. "Push him away and then draw him back in. Your problem is that you're too kind, you know that, right?"

"I thought I was shy and afraid?" Hope was fluttering in her stomach. She tried to tamp it down. It would only lead to another heart break.

Grace shook her head. "I think those are your advantages. Em is right. He'll want to save you. Just keep him guessing whether you like him in return."

Ada shook her head. Everyone had advice, but she wasn't sure any of it was going to help. Still, it might be fun to give it all a try. She knew one thing for certain, she was ready to make some changes and no man was as exciting as Blake.

"So I should make eye contact, then withdraw, lead him slowly to becoming a better man all the while teasing him with my affection and setting him to protect me?"

Grace cocked her head to one side. "Exactly."

Ada let out a huff. Was that all? No wonder she'd

been failing with men. She turned to the window, looking at the leaf buds just beginning to emerge on the trees. She knew Vice wouldn't want to be her husband but perhaps she could test a few of these theories with him? Her belly niggled with a guilt but she pushed it away. His interest was surely fleeting. He'd likely forget her before he ever realized she was using him as a learning tool.

———

VICE SHIFTED HIS WEIGHT, wondering when they were going to bloody arrive. The wind had picked up again and he was getting cold. He'd been on edge since the evening's events and he had a need to see Ada and make sure she was all right.

Finally, at the very end of the line of carriages, he spotted Daring's carriage and the Winthrops' just behind him. He straightened off the wall, weaving through the crowd to greet them as they arrived.

The moment he spied Ada, his chest tightened in the strangest way. He'd seen hundreds of debutantes all dressed in white, but none had looked as beautiful as her. Her eyes met and held his for a moment before she yanked her gaze from his.

Grace leaned over to whisper in her ear. Ada nodded several times before she peered at him again with a shy smile. And then she looked away. He wanted to hold her gaze, learn what she was thinking. Why was she keeping in suspense like this? Vice stepped up next to her. "You finally made it. I was getting worried."

Ada looked over her shoulder, directing her gaze at the woman just exiting the carriage. "Apologies. Emily decided to come after all."

Vice raised his brows. "Does Jack know she's here?"

"I don't know. Have you seen Jack?" Ada reached for his arm and his body tightened at her touch.

"He's inside," Vice muttered, leaning closer. "He looks as miserable as she does."

Ada worried her lip. "Oh dear. They don't make marriage look easy, do they?"

"They don't," he answered, grimacing. Jack had a colorful past but Vice's… his was worse. By a great deal. "There's a lesson to be learned there, I'd say."

Ada's shoulders hunched. "Surely, there is."

He turned and held out his elbow. She hesitated before placing her hand into the crook. He stared down at her. "What do you think the lesson is?"

She finally glanced at him then and held his gaze, her own eyes crinkled in question. "I suppose I thought that a man like Jack is too difficult to tame."

Vice winced. He'd been afraid of that. Ada

believed just as Camille had. He was destined to be alone. "I suppose."

"What did you mean?" She gave his arm a squeeze.

He reached over and brushed his cheek with his finger. "That honesty would have made their start much better."

Ada stopped, staring up at him. "Oh, that's much nicer than mine."

He shrugged. He understood why Jack hadn't been honest. Just the idea of confessing all his sins to a woman like Ada made his heart hammer wildly in his chest. In fact, he'd likely get through the first two and she'd run away crying never to speak with him again. "I'm not so certain. Look at what Jack's past has done to them. Imagine if she'd learned all of it before their engagement." He'd told Camille his secrets. She'd judged him rather harshly and ulti-mately left him for a better man.

Ada cocked her head to the side. "Maybe. Or perhaps it's the fact that they are secret and keep popping up to surprise her that is the issue."

"That hasn't been my experience," he muttered.

"What was your experience," she asked and then shook her head. "I'm sorry. I don't mean to pry."

They were entering through the main doors, the crush of people both making him feel watched and adding an air of privacy. "You're not. I proposed to a woman five years ago. She turned me down because my past was too colorful and my future likely to be equally so. She was right, of course. I'd just opened the club. I spent a great deal of time with men who drank heavily and gambled even more rambunctiously."

Ada's face spasmed and her other hand subtly brushed his chest. "Still. That must have hurt."

He'd been bracing himself for a barrage of questions about what exactly he'd done to earn her rejection. Ada's sympathy was like a balm he'd needed for so long. "It did."

For a moment, their eyes met. He wanted to curl up in the fresh green of her gaze but then she looked away, her arm loosening. "I should return to my family. I…"

"I'm here for you, Ada," he said, drawing her closer again. "There's no need to leave."

Staring out over the crowd. "I've my own past and it demands that I keep distance between us."

"I beg your pardon?" What past? What man? Anger swelled inside him. Who had touched Ada and how had he hurt her?

"It doesn't matter. Grace says that I shouldn't pay too much attention to you. I—" She stopped again. "I'm saying this all wrong once again."

"We'll get to Grace later. Right now, I want to know who the man in your past was."

But she'd stopped talking, stopped walking, in fact. She stumbled and he caught her, righting her back on her feet. Her face had gone pale. "Dear merciful saints," she murmured. "It's him."

With a trembling finger, she pointed into the crowd. There stood a man with dark hair and broad shoulders staring directly at his Ada. When precisely had she become his? Vice wasn't certain and it didn't matter. That man was not coming anywhere near his woman.

# CHAPTER EIGHT

ADA'S TONGUE swelled in her mouth. It was Walter. He'd left six months prior, on a mission to Africa to study wildlife, telling her he'd be gone for years. She'd never expected to see him here, tonight, at her very first event.

Without thought, she squeezed Blake's arm tighter, moving closer to him. Why was she afraid of Walter and when had Blake become her safe place?

"Who is he?" Blake's voice dropped low, a rumble making the sound gravelly.

She swallowed, then licked her lips. "He is a friend of the family."

"That isn't the entire story." Vice shifted, standing between her and Walter. "You can tell me."

She shook her head. "I lied to you the other day."

"I beg your pardon," he said as he slowly moved

them to the side, out of the crowd and away from her family.

"When I told you that I was a ruiner of rakes," she dropped her head. "I lied."

A gust of cooler air touched her skin and she realized they were making their way toward the veranda.

"That doesn't matter." He caressed her back with his fingertips. "Tell me more about your family friend."

She brushed her cheek against his arm. Somehow touching him gave her strength. "The only man who's ever shown interest in me is a biological researcher. He left six months ago for a trip to Africa and he told me not to wait for him."

"Was that man staring at you your researcher?" Vice's teeth were clenched making his words clipped but he stopped just outside the doors, in clear view of the rest of the party.

She nodded. "He wasn't supposed to come back."

"Why did he?" Vice asked, shifting her once again so that she couldn't be seen by the crowd.

"Your guess is as good as mine." She shook her head, looking up into his eyes. "I didn't know he'd returned." She placed her hands on his chest, tucking closer. "The odd thing is that I'm not certain I want to know either. I…" Even last week, she'd considered

Walter the man who had slipped through her fingers. The best she'd ever do. Now she didn't even want to speak with him.

Vice relaxed under her hands. "I would be happy to assist in any way necessary."

She nodded. Why didn't she wish to talk with Walter? He'd hurt her, that was clear. But somehow the ache was gone.

And he'd returned. Was it because of her? What if it was? She'd just amended to practice her feminine wiles. If nothing else, couldn't she try them on Walter?

But the idea filled her mouth with bile. And she realized she no longer had any feelings for him. Whatever had been between them was gone. "I don't need any assistance, but thank you, Lord Viceroy." She straightened her spine. "But I'd better return to my family. We wouldn't want to cause any more trouble this evening."

He frowned down at her before giving a quick nod and then pulled her back into the crowd. Her family was almost exactly where they'd left them and the crush of partygoers had disguised their brief disappearance, or at least, Ada hoped it had. As they rejoined her family, the group slowly made its way to the opposite end of the ballroom where they found a small space and a few empty chairs.

Vice had gone silent but he remained at her side, her hand tucked in his elbow. For Ada's part, she was lost in thought and happy for the pillar of strength currently holding her aloft in the crowd.

Did she go speak to Walter, pretend he wasn't there? Inhaling deeply, she drew in Blake's rich scent. It was comforting and exciting and she found herself brushing her cheek against him once again.

He leaned his head down, his chin brushing the top of her head. Ada's eyes fluttered closed. "I wish I could just leave. I don't want to be here."

Blake smiled against the top of her head. "Me too."

"I'm interrupting," another man said from next to her. She left her eyes closed. Walter. Her stomach twisted and she moved closer to Vice, drawing in Vice's scent, the feel of his heat next to hers.

Slowly, she lifted her head and opened her eyes. Part of her wished to say yes he was interrupting, but she'd been raised to be polite. "Of course not, Mr. Conroy." She looked at Vice, whose face had gone hard. "May I introduce you to Lord Viceroy."

Walter gave a quick jerk of his chin. "My lord."

"Mr. Conroy," Vice replied, his voice hard and flat. Ada, without thinking, gave his arm another squeeze. Touching him calmed her. Soothed her jagged nerves.

Blake looked down, his eyes crinkling in a question. Then he glanced up again. "I'd ask how you and Miss Chase know one another but she's told me about you already. The question now is why are you back in England?"

Walter straightened. "I have unfinished business here," he answered. Then he stepped closer. "Miss Chase, may I ask for a dance?"

Ada looked to Vice, whose face had turned to granite once again. His jaw was tense and a muscle jumped in his temple. She had no grounds, however, to refuse. "Of course."

"Very good. I'll take the next." He reached for her card, then wrote in his name before he positioned himself on Ada's other side. She drew in a breath, not sure what to make of it. As she looked at him, he turned toward her. "The dance will begin in just a few minutes. It seems silly to leave and return in this crowd." He glared at Vice. "And I'd enjoy extra time in your company."

Ada swallowed. Well, this was a bit sticky. Grace sauntered by, giving her an exaggerated wink. "It's working already," she said in a loud whisper.

"What's working?" Blake asked as he shifted her closer.

"I have no idea," she answered, finally dropping her hand from his arm. Ada had never expected to be positioned between two men. A giggle bubbled up in her chest. While she didn't want Walter anymore, she may as well enjoy her one night of having multiple beaux. And Grace was correct. She couldn't give Vice all her affection. He'd only break her heart. It was time to put a little distance between them. "Tell me all about your journey, Mr. Conroy."

———

VICE STOOD ABSOLUTELY STILL, using every ounce of his energy not to punch Walter Conroy directly in the face. Everything inside him screamed to pull Ada close and make this man disappear. But then what? Would she be stuck with Vice?

Jealousy coated the inside of his mouth. This man was pulling Ada away from him. Conroy'd had his chance with Ada, had literally sailed halfway around the world. The man should have stayed gone.

"I got on that ship, Miss Chase, and realized what a terrible mistake I'd made. I should never have left you."

Vice heard Ada's gasp. Damn Conroy. Damn himself for not being a better man. Conroy was likely honorable and upstanding. All the things a man named Vice lacked. He hated himself in this moment. Even worse, he knew if he cared for Ada at all, he should step aside and allow Conroy to court her. Vice wanted to hit something. Anything.

"When we reached the first port in Northern Africa, I left the ship and found another to return home but it was a merchant vessel and made several stops." He stepped closer to Ada, taking her hand. "I know I've been gone six months and I know I told you not to wait but..." Conroy brought her hand to his lips and kissed her gloved skin.

Vice's skin crawled with tingling energy. His fists clenched and unclenched. Yes. He definitely wanted to punch the researcher.

"Oh Walter, you don't need to apologize. It was—"

"I want to." Walter stopped her. "I wish I'd stayed. I wish that I'd asked you to marry me."

"What?" The word left her lips in a gasp as Vice's insides twisted in pain. It was going to happen again. He was going to lose another woman to a better man. He should never allow himself to care. He'd worked so hard to have the perfect relationships on the outside that were devoid of any emotion.

"You don't mean that," Ada said. "Your work, it takes you—"

"I know what the job requires. What I need to ask you, is can you be part of that with me?"

94

"I," Ada started, her hand still resting in both of his. "I'm not—"

"Our dance is beginning." Conroy tucked her hand into his elbow. "Let's go, my love."

Vice jolted, his lip curling over his teeth. Conroy gave him a wary glance over Ada's head as he pulled her into the crowd. Vice's heart ached in his chest watching that man pull her away. Ada should be next to him not with Conroy. But he pushed that thought back down. Ada should be with the man who could make her happy. Vice had never fulfilled anyone, not even himself.

"Mother fu—" Vice started but a tap at his shoulder stopped him. He turned to see Ada's cousin standing to his right.

"There is a lady present," Grace said, giving him an angelic smile.

He glared at her, then realized how harsh his expression must be and attempted to relax the muscles of his face. "Apologies," he mumbled, his body still vibrating with anger.

Grace's smile widened. "Upset, are we?"

He drew in an unsteady breath, trying to clear his head. "That man is—"

Grace raised a brow. "All wrong for Ada."

Vice narrowed his gaze. "Are you saying that to fill in my thought or is it your own?"

Grace shrugged. "It's my own." Then she lifted her finger. "But I'm not sure I approve of you either." And then she tapped him on the shoulder again. "What are your intentions toward Ada?"

"Intentions? I have none other than to do as I've been directed and follow her about like a puppy." He was lying. About all of it. He wanted to keep her for his own, he knew that now. But he also wanted her to have the man she deserved. Since the death of his parents he'd been broken. Camille had known it and Ada would realize it soon enough.

Grace's lips thinned. He had to confess, he'd never seen this side of her. He was a touch intimidated. "I'm not going to insult either of us by pointing out all the ways in which you are far more dangerous than a puppy. Nor will I point out how I know you have intentions. What I've yet to understand is how honorable they are."

"I don't know what you mean?" He sought out Ada on the dance floor. Conroy was swinging her effortlessly about, looking supremely confident. Vice scowled again, his chest constricting. He didn't have the energy for this conversation.

"You know what I mean. You're a rake. You think too highly of yourself. You don't want to marry and you're far too handsy with my cousin. Am I right?"

Bad had stepped in just behind Grace and he

heard his friend chuckle. Vice looked away from Ada to stare at Bad. "You stay out of it," he called over Grace's shoulder. Bad only laughed the harder. He focused his attention back on Ada's cousin. "If you think all that about me, why are we talking?"

"You like her," Grace said. "And when she is with you..." Grace scrunched up her nose, shifting her weight. "She...well, she is her most vivacious self." She raised one shoulder. "She doesn't even trip about when she's near you, which when I think about it, is very interesting indeed."

Vice's mouth fell open. Could that be true? "You think I am good for her?"

Grace shrugged. "Better than him. Did you see how he never even lets her speak? With you, she fights, she laughs, she pushes. I like seeing her like that. But," then Grace poked him, hard, "if you ruin her than I shall be forced to have Daring and Bad—"

"Bad is going to side with you over me?" Vice looked back at his friend who had stopped laughing.

Grace looked back at the baron as well. "Bad?" She gave him a sweet smile, the sort that lit her entire face.

Bad blinked several times, his face filled with a longing that Vice had never seen. Bad had kept quiet about Grace but in this moment, Vice wondered if his friend was falling in love. "I'll see that Vice behaves."

It was Vice's turn to laugh. Partially because Bad was being led around by the nose, but mostly at himself. "I've no intention of doing anything that would compromise Ada." He meant every word, which shocked him to no end.

"Do you plan to marry her then?" Grace crossed her arms. "Because you're paying her a great deal of attention and my family is beginning to notice."

Vice grimaced, looking down at the floor. "Ada would make a fine wife. I, however, for several reasons, lack the merits to be a good husband."

Grace paused and Bad stepped closer. "I understand that completely," his friend answered quietly.

Vice shook his head. "But if you say he isn't good for her then I can help her with this." In fact, he'd take great pleasure in getting rid of Walter Conroy.

# CHAPTER NINE

ADA SPUN ABOUT THE FLOOR, trying to catch Vice's eye. Walter had been talking without pause. "We'll marry, of course, and then you could travel to Africa with me. We'll have to be careful not to conceive until we return to London, but at least we'll be together."

Part of her liked his words and she found herself softening underneath his touch. She'd felt so rejected and his plans soothed her ego. "You've thought it all out."

"I have, Ada. Time on a ship can do that to you." He pulled her closer and she stiffened in his arms. "I can take care of you. I can love you."

It was lovely to hear but it wasn't in her nature to allow him to continue just to feel better about herself. He could love her, but how could she reciprocate when someone else had captured her heart? "Walter." The single word was quiet but firm.

He hesitated for a moment, his eyes growing weary, before he continued. "With this last trip, I could spend years working here in London, publishing journals, giving lectures. We could build a life, Ada. I know I left you once but I've come back to prove to you that I can be the man you need. Come to Africa with me. Just for a few years. We can—"

She shook her head. "No." The word came out harsher than she'd intended but if she wasn't direct, he might run away with the conversation again. Which was one of the reasons he'd never be the man she wanted.

"Don't say that." He held her waist tighter. "It took me months to come back here. At least give me a chance."

She winced. "Try to understand. Without you here, I did a great deal of thinking and—"

"It's that viscount, isn't it?" His lip curled. "I saw the way you leaned into him. You're in public and you're not promised to him. How could you act like that?"

Ada cleared her throat. "It isn't Blake."

"Blake?" They were turning faster. "It's Blake

now? How long have you known him? Did you begin courting the moment I left?"

Ada tried to pull away, but Walter held her firm. "I think you should release me."

His face hardened, his neck bulging with tendons and muscles. "I've been on a ship for six months to get back to you and now—"

"That isn't true," she snapped. "You spent at least half of it leaving me here to wonder why you didn't care enough about me to stay. You never wrote me a letter or sent me a postcard."

Walter pulled his chin back, his features going slack. "That's fair. But I see the error in my ways now."

She shook her head. "It's too late."

"No." They were moving toward the doors to the hall. "It isn't too late. I refuse to accept that."

She tried to plant her feet but he overpowered her and her feet tangled in her skirts. He dragged her against him, pulling her toward the doors. "Walter. Stop. I don't want to dance anymore."

"Neither do I. You and I need to talk about several subjects, all of which require privacy."

That filled her with fear. She did not want to be alone with this man at this moment or any. He might ruin her. Anger emanated off him in waves and she attempted to pull away again. "No. I must insist you return me to my family."

"You can't tell me you haven't been alone with him. I see how comfortable you are touching him." He spun her right out the doors. She didn't have much choice, glancing around him she met Blake's gaze, which was fixed on her. Just before her view of Vice would be cut off, she mouthed a single word. *Help.* She didn't doubt for a moment that he'd come. Somehow, she knew Vice would always come for her.

Walter stopped dancing, dragging her down the hall. "I love you, Ada. I've loved you for years." He pulled faster. "I wish I'd stayed and married you, but don't tell me I'm going to lose you to that dandy of a lord. I need to prove to you that I'm the better man." He began trying doors as they continued down the hall, his hand about her upper arm in a tight grip. She tried to tug away but he was too strong.

Desperation rolled off him in waves, and fear made Ada choke out a sob. She grasped at his shirt, desperate to say anything that would make him change course. "You're not losing me to him." She attempted to pull him to a stop but once again failed. "He isn't the marrying sort." She knew the words were wrong the second they left her mouth. She did that when she was nervous.

And she felt the shift in Walter. He was a strong man, but his grip turned to stone. Walter pushed open a door, then pulled her inside, whipping her around. "Then why reject my offer? I would make you my wife." And then he pulled her against his body and lowered his mouth toward hers. "Ada, I need to show you the depth of my affection."

Everything inside her screamed in denial. She'd never kissed a man and this couldn't be her first. Not like this. She knew Walter was hurt but that didn't give him the right to take this from her. Her insides tightened as she yanked backward, dropped her shoulder, and heaved it into his stomach. She heard his whoosh of breath and for a moment she thought she was free.

Victory sang in her veins and, pulling back, she lunged for the door but he grabbed her sleeve and held tight even as the fabric ripped. "Ada," he grated out. "We need to finish this conversation. I'm not done."

She drew in a breath, still trying to squirm away as her dress made several more ripping sounds. "Let go," she cried.

The door flew open nearly hitting her. She stopped, staring as Blake marched into the room. His face was drawn into tight lines, his chest puffed out. "You heard her. Let go."

"This isn't your concern," Walter growled back. "Get out of here and let us work out-—"

Vice's answer was to raise his fist and plant it directly into Walter's nose. Suddenly, she was free and she stumbled to the side, bumping into the wall. Whirling about, she watched Vice hit Walter again. Walter tried to swing back but he missed and Blake raised his fist a third time. "Don't," she cried, raising her hand.

Blake held his fist in place. "He tried to hurt you."

Trembling, she pushed off the wall. "He was hurting too." Then she reached out a trembling hand to touch his arm. "No more violence. Please, Blake, just escort Mr. Conroy outside. It's time for him to leave."

Blake didn't take his eyes off Walter as he grabbed the other man by the collar and began hauling him toward the door. "Stay here," he barked. Walter was doubled over, holding his nose, which poured out blood, as Blake dragged him from the room. She looked at her dress. The sleeve ripped off and hung down her arm. What was she going to do?

———

VICE GROWLED with satisfaction as he tossed Conroy

into the gravel drive. "I don't want to see you anywhere near Ada ever again."

Walter was still holding his nose, pinching it closed to stem the blood. "She'll choose me, you know. In the end, she'll choose me."

"You've lost your wits. You just attacked her." Vice clenched his fists again, wishing he'd hit the man several more times. Only Ada's request held him back.

"She understands. You heard her. And she understands you too. You know what she said? You're not the marrying kind. She doesn't want to marry you." Walter stumbled to the side, hailing one of the servants. "My carriage."

Vice clenched his jaw but inside his stomach sank. Of course Ada thought he wasn't the marrying kind. What woman of worth would want him?

He thought back to his list of accomplished women. All of them had been too preoccupied with their own successes to notice his deficiencies. That was the real reason he picked the experienced women with no strings attached. There was never a real connection with any of them.

Spinning about, he stomped up the steps, and back into the house. Making his way down the hall, he opened the door to the room where he'd left Ada. He could see now that it was a study with a large desk and shelves upon shelves of books. Ada stood exactly where he'd left her, hugging her arms about herself.

Any anger he might have felt melted. Her dress was terribly torn, her face streaked with tears.

Softly closing the door, he crossed over to her and gently pulled her into his arms. She melted into him.

"Blake," she said, her voice trembling. "What am I going to do? Look at my dress."

He held her closer. "We'll sort all that out. Are you all right? Did he hurt you?" She was so soft in his arms, her honey smell wafting into his nostrils.

"I'm fine. My dress got the worst of the damage." She looked down, touching her ripped sleeve. "My mother is going to—" Her eyes flew to his. "You don't think she'll force me to marry Walter, do you?"

He gathered her closer. "I'll murder him first."

"Blake." Her eyes widened as she stared up at him. "You wouldn't."

"Fine. Not murder. Perhaps castration? He can't marry if he doesn't have—"

This time her mouth snapped closed. "Blake."

He cupped her cheek, his thumb running along her lips. "I'll not allow them to force you into a match with him, I swear it."

She pressed a small kiss on the pad of his thumb.

His cock swelled at the light touch. "Thank you," she breathed against the sensitive flesh of his finger. "Can I ask you one more favor?"

"Of course," he answered, his voice getting deeper with his growing awareness.

She kissed the sensitive webbing between his thumb and forefinger. "I thought that Walter was going to steal my first kiss." She rubbed her nose along the inside of his hand, placing another light peck on his palm.

"I would have had to kill him then," he answered, his breath coming in shallow gasps. Not because of his anger. Her light kisses were wreaking havoc on his body.

"Stop talking about violence." She nibbled a path to his wrist.

His heart beat rapidly in his chest. Never had such small touches affected him so much. "Fine." He slid his other hand up her arm and over her neck, cupping her jaw and tilting Ada's head so that he could look into her eyes. "What do you want to ask?"

She swallowed then, her delicate throat working. "I want you to kiss me."

He stopped, searching her face. He didn't want to ask why, didn't want to think about what this meant. He needed that kiss. "Ask and you shall receive."

## CHAPTER TEN

ADA KNEW IT WAS UNWISE. If caught, they'd be married for certain. In fact, even now, being alone like this…

But something had shifted. When Walter had tried to steal that kiss, well, she fought him because she wanted to give her first experience away to a man who made her heart thrum in her chest. And that man was Blake.

With aching deliberateness, Blake reached for her face, cupping her cheeks in his palms as his thumbs made tiny circles at her temples. "Ada," he groaned, searching her face as he leaned a bit closer. "Are you certain?"

"Yes," she whispered, drifting closer to him. The world had slowed to an unhurried pace which only made her that much more excited, as if part of the joy was to be found in savoring the moment. "I've never wanted anything more."

He groaned deep in his throat. A small noise that was almost imperceptible to the ear but it vibrated through her, settling deep in her core and causing her to ache between her legs.

"Close your eyes," he whispered, his lips but a breath away, so close, she could nearly feel them, or was she imagining the sensation?

"I don't think I want to," she said, lifting up on her tiptoes and sliding her arms around his waist. "I would hate to miss one single bit of this."

One side of his mouth lifted in a smile. "Trust me, love. You'll feel all the more without your sight."

She blinked twice, then closed her lids, trusting him to lead her where she belonged. In answer he placed his lips over hers. Just a soft brush, nothing more, but she gasped in response, drawing back and opening her eyes. "Blake," she said as her lips parted and she stared into his eyes. "That was so…"

One of his hands slid down her neck, causing shivers to run all over her body. "Dreadful?"

It was her turn to smile. "Delicious."

"That's a much better word." He slid his fingers into the back of her hair, massaging her scalp. "That hair," he said, his voice rough and craggy. "It's so silky. I want to see it undone."

Ada gave her head a small shake. That couldn't happen, of course. This was just a kiss but he didn't give her a chance to say so, his lips pressing against hers again. This kiss was firmer than the last, stronger, and more satisfying. She squeezed him tighter as he pressed her lips closed than lifted his mouth to do the same action over again and then again.

She could barely catch a breath when he slanted her mouth open rather than closed, his tongue sliding along her bottom lip.

Never had she imagined such pleasure and her knees buckled as she moaned into his mouth.

Blake jerked back, staring down at her. "Ada?"

"What?" She stiffened worried she'd done something wrong. Had she been too enthusiastic?

"Love. You can't make noises like that," he said, sliding his hand down her chest just above her breast. The skin of her nipple tightened in anticipation but he skimmed his palm under her arm and down her side to her waist.

"I'm sorry if I offended. I'll try—"

"Ada," Blake groaned. "You didn't offend me. Noises like that make me want so much more. But this kiss, it's for you."

"Oh," she answered as she looked into his blue eyes. In the candlelight they looked darker, just flecks of blue shimmering as the light moved. How could one man be so stunning? "I'll do my best but I didn't expect one kiss to be so…"

"Delicious?" He smiled, stroking her cheek, jaw, then chin. "It was more than that, though, love. It was incredibly—"

The door banged open and they both turned to see a couple fervently embracing as they stumbled into the room.

"I love you," the woman murmured, her lips crushed to her partner's.

"Emily?" Ada asked, coming around to Blake's side.

Emily broke away from Jack turning to her cousin. "Ada?" Emily's eyes widened as she took in the scene, her mouth falling open. "What's going on?"

Ada instantly realized her mistake. She was alone with Blake at her very first ball. "Don't tell mother. I promise it was all very innocent. I—"

"Your dress!" Emily pointed at the sleeve. Then she snapped her gaze to Blake. "You!" Without warning she rushed at Blake, pulling her skirts near to her knees. "Get away from my cousin."

She came at him in a flurry of petticoats and flailing hands. "You devil. I knew you were no good but to have accosted a sweet, innocent girl like—"

Each word was punctuated by a smack in Blake's face.

"Emily." Ada tried to block Emily's flailing hands as Blake put up an arm to protect himself. "I'm not a girl and Blake didn't—" But she didn't get to finish either. Jack rushed in behind his wife.

"Vice, we trusted you," Jack said, reaching his arm over his wife's shoulder to push Vice.

That made Emily bump into him causing Ada to tilt off kilter and lean her weight into his side. He tipped backwards, stumbling on a chair. His arm was still around Ada and they both tumbled to the side, falling toward the ground.

Blake yanked her against his front, smacking his back into the floor as her weight landed on top of him. He gave a loud grunt as her body pressed into his, hers perfectly cushioned. "Bloody bullocks, Jack," he yelled out. "What did you do that for? You could have hurt Ada."

"I could have hurt, Ada?" Jack snapped back. "That's ripe. And you'll pay for this." Jack moved toward them, his face twisted in anger.

Ada buried her face into Jack's chest, gripping his shoulders. "Stop," she called, though the sound was muffled. "Blake didn't rip my dress, Walter Conroy did."

"What?" Jack stopped.

Emily called behind him, "What?"

"Blake was attempting to help me delicately get out of this situation. The last thing I need is for mother to demand I marry Walter." She squeezed her eyes shut, burrowing deeper against Blake, who held her tight to him.

He kissed the top of her head. "I told you. I won't allow that to happen. If it comes to that, I'll marry you myself. Your mother will surely approve of a Viscount over Mr. Conroy."

This time Emily and Jack spoke in absolute unison. "What?"

———

THE WORDS LEFT his mouth before he'd thought them out. He clamped his teeth together. What had he just done?

Ada lifted her head from where it was burrowed in his chest and her green eyes met his, her mauve lips parted in question. "Blake."

Her little tongue darted out to wet her lips, the one he hadn't actually been able to taste since they'd been interrupted. He knew he wanted to, desperately wished to sample the nectar that was her mouth. "I know what you're going to say. You don't want a man like me."

Her brows drew together in question. "That wasn't what I was going to say."

Jack stepped up next to them. "I am sorry that I pushed you. But I think we need to wait to have this conversation. How long has Ada been in here?"

A muscle jumped in Vice's jaw. Too long. "A quarter hour, perhaps longer."

Jack grimaced. "Wrap her in your coat, then you and Emily can take her out to the carriage. I will tell her family that…" He paused. "What should I tell them?"

"Tell them I was sick. Nausea." Ada's nervous temperament often meant her stomach bothered her. "They'll believe you."

Ada started to straighten. He didn't want to let her go. For a second more he held her close and then with a grumble of dissatisfaction, he sat up with her in his arms. He could have lifted her but Jack reached down his hand and pulled her to standing, Vice following.

Taking off his coat, he draped the heavy fabric over her shoulders. Her hair was loose, thanks to his fingers. He winced even as his fingers itched to pull out those pins and let the tresses fall around him like waves of light. "Emily, we'll take her out the back."

Emily nodded and started for the door. "I'll make certain no one is coming. She can't be seen like this."

Emily peaked her head out and then called back. "The hall is empty."

Vice pulled at the lapels of his coat as Ada started after her cousin. Jack reached for Vice's arm. "A word of advice." Jack leaned closer. "Just marry her."

Vice frowned. "No offense, but I'm not certain that's the correct path. Have you considered that we aren't meant for…" He stopped, not wanting to insult his friend.

Jack shook his head. "I made one critical error that I've corrected. There are no more lies between us. No half-truths. Learn from me and you'll be fine. And if you're still in doubt, watch Daring. He's as good at marriage as he is everything else."

Vice gave a quick nod as he followed Ada, tucking his arm about her. Her body fit so perfectly against his as he cupped the curve of her waist that he wished he could mold them together. Her sweet scent of honey wrapped about him and a piece of her hair fell from her coif, trailing down his arm.

Marry her?

What would that be like? First, he thought of her in his bed every night. Bloody hell, his cock strained against the falls of his breeches.

Then he considered the days. Her gentle smile, kind words, her smell permeating his home. But what about her? How would she feel when she learned all the women who had traipsed over those very same floors?

They made their way down the back stairwell and out into the alley where carriages lined the street. Reluctantly, he let Ada go and stepped in front of Emily. Not seeing his vehicle, he walked to the curb, hailing a hack.

The ladies hustled out into the street, climbing in the small carriage. "I can take her home from here," Emily said as she leaned out the door. "Thank you."

His lips thinned as Ada disappeared from view. He didn't want to let her go but then she leaned back out again. Her mouth trembled and her eyes held his as though she were looking for something. "I'm staying at my aunt and uncle's."

He gave a single nod and then shut the door. He already missed the feel of her pressed to his side.

It made sense that he stayed. He'd return inside, make a turnabout the room. Have it be known that he'd never left the party. But he'd rather be in that carriage with her.

She'd told him she was staying with Lord and Lady Winthrop. Did she hope he'd visit? Excitement burst inside him at the thought of seeing her again.

Trotting back down the alley, he made his way inside and back up the stairs. The ball was now in full swing, the crowd swirling about the floor. He inched around the edge, finding the Chase family. Bad stood with them, his eyes glued to the dance floor. He followed his friend's gaze until he saw Grace being twirled about in another man's arms. Was Bad doing his duty as guard or was there something more in his friend's dark gaze?

Tonight, Vice couldn't ask. Instead, he weaved through the family to arrive at Mr. Chase's side.

"My lord," Mr. Chase bowed his head.

Vice nodded back. "Mr. Chase."

"How does Ada fare?" Her father was staring at the dance floor as well.

He swallowed. "Just a bit sick, sir. Nothing to concern yourself over."

"I know that Conroy pulled her into the hall, I saw him and I saw you go after them." The man straightened, drawing to his full height. "Anything I should be concerned about?"

His heart stopped. "No sir. I made sure he won't bother her again."

"Good," her father answered, then he turned to look at Vice. "You remind me of myself at your age. Before I met Winnifred."

Vice raised his brows. "Thank you?"

Mr. Chase focused on the dance floor again a bit of a grin curving his lips. "I was quite the rogue."

"I beg your pardon." Vice started, taking a partial step back.

Mr. Chase held up his hand. "I put those days behind me long ago. The question is, are you ready for the same fate?"

Vice drew in a deep breath. "Yes, sir. I believe I am." Had he really just said that? He pictured Ada and his eyes drifted closed. "But I am unsure that I am worthy of her."

"Ahh." Mr. Chase slapped him on the back. "Come see me tomorrow. Ten sharp. If you'd be so inclined, we'll take Grace and Ada ribbon shopping afterward. Grace is not the sort of woman that likes to be kept waiting."

Vice gave a single nod. "Lord Baderness will want to join us."

"Fine," the other man answered. "Now go home and get some sleep. Tomorrow will be a big day."

Vice turned to go. What Mr. Chase said was certainly true. He'd already asked a woman to marry him once. He wasn't certain he was looking forward to asking a second. The question was, would it be a wonderful day or a terrible one?

# CHAPTER ELEVEN

ADA SAT in the carriage with Emily, looking at her cousin. "You and Jack? Were you kissing?"

Emily leaned forward. "Don't worry about me now. You're the one we need to focus on tonight."

"Trust me, I want to know. Did the two of you make up?" Ada reached out and took her cousins hand.

Emily gave her a glowing smile. "Yes. We did. Thank goodness."

"Do you think you'll fight like that again?" Ada swallowed.

Sitting back in her seat, Emily shook her head. "I'm sure we'll fight. All couples fight. Don't they?"

"I suppose they do." Ada sat back. "I'm asking because I see a lot of commonalities between Jack and Blake."

Emily nodded. "Me too." She tapped her chin. "Former rogues."

Ada held up her hand. "I'd say that Blake is a current rogue."

"He offered to marry you to save you," Emily answered.

Ada's insides twisted. That should make her happy, but somehow, it hurt. "It was a contingent offer."

Emily frowned. "That's true. But I never pictured him making any sort of offer at all. So you're clearly making progress."

Ada paused. "Mother said that I was the sort that could lead a man to change so slowly, he wouldn't even know it was happening."

Emily grinned. "I love that and I think it's true. Vice is like a different man when he's with you."

"And the other man? The man he still is with everyone else? What do I do with him?" Ada stared out the window as her stomach dropped again.

"He'll get smaller and smaller," Emily said. "Do you know why I was angry at Jack?"

"He lied," Ada answered, not really thinking about it. Her thoughts were busy contemplating Vice and his other half. When they were together, she forgot to be afraid, but when they weren't, she remembered the man he was. The man who would grow bored with a little mouse for a wife.

"No, that's only part of it."

"What?" Ada turned to her cousin.

"I was angry because I can forgive his past but I've a much more difficult time when he makes those same mistakes in the present. Don't judge Vice on who he was, take him for who he can become."

"And what if neither man wants a woman like me in the long term?" Ada bit her lip. "I'm not exciting like you and Grace, or strong like Minnie and Diana, or smart like Cordelia. I'm..." She paused, looking for the word.

"You are positively wonderful." Emily touched her knee. "Honestly, you bring out the best in everyone around you and that includes him. Don't doubt that."

Ada didn't respond as she struggled to find words. Did Emily really think that?

The carriage pulled up to her aunt and uncle's home, and she and Emily climbed out. It was only then she realized that she still wore Blake's jacket. Pulling the garment tighter about herself, she dropped her nose into it and drew in a deep breath. Inhaling his unique scent, her insecurities drifted away as her body tightened in response.

"The thing is, Ada," Emily said as she finished

paying the driver and began to climb the steps. "Marriage is always a leap of faith. And even now, I haven't quite decided if I've made the right one. Stop asking yourself if you're good enough. Instead, ask if he is what you really want."

She drew in a quick breath. She knew the answer to that question. It was so simple. "Yes. He is."

Emily gave her a large smile. "See. Admitting the truth wasn't so hard, was it?"

Ada shook her head. Knowing she wanted him was the easy part. The much harder task would be convincing him to marry her and then holding his interest. But Emily was right. If he was the man for her then catching him was worth trying.

———

THE NEXT DAY, Vice trotted up the stairs to Ada's home, not that she was there. He wished she were. Seeing her would make this day so much easier.

He'd hardly slept last night, worrying about the details of today and beyond. How should he ask? Would she say yes? How would he convince her over time that he could become a man worthy of her affection?

Knocking on the brass knocker, the door swung open almost instantly. But it wasn't the butler or even Mr. Chase who greeted him but Jack. "What the...?"

Jack grimaced. "I'm not happy about it either. I had plans this morning to move my wife back into my house. Instead, I have been coerced into leading a party of ribbon-shoppers."

"Seriously?" Vice squinted his eyes. "Mr. Chase isn't going to attend?"

"Sick," Jack answered with a deepening frown. "I have a feeling the man may have dove too deeply into his cups last night. He's a bit of a drinker. Always has been. And he seemed to be celebrating another successful match." Jack's brows rose. "He also said that you have his blessing, whatever that means." Jack gave him a pointed stare. "And that you are to make sure Lord Baderness is appropriate."

Vice's lips parted in surprise. He'd been given responsibilities in the family. "Shall we then?"

"In a moment," Jack pointed down the drive. "Here comes Bad now." Then he scratched his head. "Not very long ago we were staying up all hours of the night running a secret club. Now we're off on a ribbon-hunting adventure before noon. The worst part, I'm excited. I've hardly gotten to see my wife in days and I would follow her into a sea of taffeta if it meant I got a single kiss."

Vice shook his head. "I'd allow myself to get

knocked down every day, much like you did last night, if it meant Ada would look at me with that adoring gaze. I'm a slave."

"You're not a slave, my friend, you're just in love." Jack smacked his back. "Come on. Let's go. We've got women to drool over."

Vice followed Jack. On the surface that hadn't changed. They'd always drooled over women. And yet, their lives couldn't be more different. Love? Had Jack actually just used that word? And even more alarming, Jack might be right. He'd never felt this way about anyone. Not ever. His heart thrummed with the emotion, overwhelming his senses. "Do you think you'll grow tired of being married?"

"You've witnessed mine and Emily's relationship, have you not? Bored is the last thing I'll be."

Bad hopped out of his carriage staring at his two friends. "Ribbon shopping?" He puffed out his chest. "Did I ever tell you that I survived by fighting in street fights?"

"No," Vice answered, skidding to a stop. Was that what Crusher had been referring to? "You were a fighter? Before you inherited the title?" He glanced up and down Bad's face. "No wonder your skin looks like it's been through a meat grinder." He didn't mean it as an insult. He forgot sometimes that Bad has a difficult upbringing.

Bad scowled, his face settling into deep lines of dissatisfaction. "You're an ass. And Grace is a pain. Now I'm following around a spoiled little princess as she hunts for the perfect shade of blue ribbon." He threw up his hands. "All of us, our days destroyed at her whim."

Vice cocked an eyebrow. "Is that really what you're angry at? I saw you watching her dance with Lord Williams."

Bad raised a fist. "Don't test me."

Vice held up his hands. "Sorry. I'll stay out of it. I've got my own problems."

"He does." Jack grinned as he looped an arm about Vice's neck. "He's in love."

Vice's cheeks heated but Bad looked as though he'd been struck but lightning. "Not you too?"

"I haven't bandied about that word," he replied, giving a shrug. "But I'm beginning to wonder…"

Bad scrubbed his scalp with his hands disheveling his hair and making his appearance even more outrageously dark. "I don't want to know."

Vice squinted one eye, assessing Bad. His friend always had a cool and controlled exterior. But not today. Perhaps Vice wasn't the only one being affected by a Chase woman. Bad had been acting strangely indeed. "Fine. Let's get this over with then, shall we?"

"Yes, please." Bad climbed into Vice's larger carriage. "Tonight we are heading back out to see if we can find Abernath again. I want this business over with and that detective Daring hired isn't doing the job nearly quick enough."

"I agree with that sentiment." He did want the business with Abernath done. Ada, however, he hoped he was just beginning with her. "Ada needs to be safe and—"

"Bloody hell, you are in love." Bad tossed himself back against the seat. "We'll have to sell the club. I can't run it by myself, even with Sin's help."

Vice stared at his friend. Sell the club? Did he want that? The club was the entire reason he'd agreed to watch over Ada in the first place.

But when he thought of his future, he didn't see participating in any more late nights out with drunk men. He rather pictured them curled in bed with auburn hair trailing over his chest. "Let's tackle the first problem, then we can figure out the fate of the Den of Sins."

Bad let out a groan. "I think I hoped that you would deny the need to sell the place."

Vice shrugged but it was Jack who spoke. "A gaming hell is a young single man's enterprise. We are getting older."

Bad stared out the window, his brow drawn low. "You are, perhaps. I've only just begun living my life."

The men fell silent. In a few minutes they'd reached the Winthrop Estate and Jack went inside to fetch the ladies. He forgot all about his worry the moment that Ada stepped into the carriage. She wore a gown of ivory, setting off her creamy skin and flashing green eyes. He wanted to pull her in his lap but she sat in the seat across from him, giving him a small smile. "Good afternoon."

"Hello," he replied. He wanted to say so much more than that. Maybe confess his feelings. Kiss her senseless or...his breath caught in his throat. He wished to beg her to give him a chance.

He thought back to Camille. He hadn't begged. He'd been young and hurt, and he'd stormed away to leave her family to pack. But Ada...he wasn't above pleading. She was a softer woman, and...he leaned closer as she stared back. She was the sort of woman who could fill a man with love.

"Ada," he started.

"Don't," Bad croaked. "Not here. Not now."

Vice grimaced. Whatever Bad was struggling with, he was sorry for his friend. But he wouldn't allow it to get in his way today. Today was the day he convinced Ada to be his, no matter the consequences. He still didn't know if he was the right man for her but he couldn't give her up either. He could only hope her heart was kind enough to accept him despite his flaws. Vice understood he was appealing to her pity, but he'd take that over watching her marry someone else.

## CHAPTER TWELVE

ADA LOOKED at Blake with narrowed eyes. Something was different about him today. Intensity rolled off him in waves, and his stare didn't waver once.

She shifted, clasping her hands together. Last night he'd been tender, gentle. Today, however, there was an energy about him that made her feel…invigorated. Her pulse raced, blood singing in her veins. "Where is my father?"

"Ill after last night," Jack answered, climbing into the carriage. "He sent me in his stead."

Ada pressed her lips together. The original rake, he'd likely overindulged last eve. Her mother would nurse her father back to wellness once again. She always did.

She looked over at Vice. Was that what would

happen with her? Like her mother, would she tame her rake into a family man who had the occasional bouts of excess?

Ada nibbled her lip. What was she asking this question for? He'd only marry her if Walter forced the issue. Unless she could convince him otherwise. Was that even possible?

"Bad," Grace said from her seat next to Ada. "What ribbon shop should we go to first?"

Bad choked. "There is more than one?"

Grace flitted her hand. "Of course. Ribbons are an important accessory. Don't you know that?"

Bad's lips thinned as they pulled over his teeth. "What I know is that Jack and Emily, and Ada and Vice, along with myself, have all had their days ruined so that you can pick out a scrap of fabric that you likely don't need. Don't you feel the least bit of remorse?"

"I beg your pardon?" Grace sat up straighter, her face turning bright red. "I've been trapped in the house for weeks, thanks to your lot."

Bad pointed his finger. "You're the one who arrived uninvited to a gentleman's club in the middle of the night."

Grace squeaked out a sound of irritation. "That wasn't my idea. In fact, I didn't want to go and I wish I'd listened to myself." She leaned over and poked

Bad in the shoulder. "If I had, I wouldn't be in danger and I wouldn't need to find a husband post haste because you lot are so bloody terrible at finding one single woman."

Then she flounced back into her seat.

The carriage rolled to a stop and Bad launched from his place toward the door. "If you need me, I'll be at the tavern."

"Which tavern?" Jack asked crinkling his brow.

"Whichever one is closest," Bad answered, hoping from the carriage and slamming the door behind him.

Grace sniffed. "Good riddance."

But Ada wasn't so certain. "Grace," she reached for her cousin. "Going out is dangerous enough. We should have a man for every woman—"

"Ada," Grace snapped back. "I don't need your nervous little tweeting now. For goodness sake, stop being afraid all the time. It's ridiculous."

Ada winced, her shoulders hunching in embarrassment. She wasn't just being nervous, she simply wanted to keep Grace safe. Vice leaned forward, touching her knee with his palm. She swallowed, her gaze meeting his as she placed her hand on top of his. She straightened back up. He'd certainly help her, which made Ada smile.

"It isn't," Vice cut in. "We flushed Abernath out

last night. Despite your comment, catching one woman in a city full of thousands is difficult. But she knows we're on to her and honestly, it would be safer for you to return home. I'm worried how she might retaliate."

Ada's breath caught in her throat. They'd been chasing Lady Abernath at night? She was both proud and frightened.

"No," Grace snapped back, also standing. "I am not determining what I do with my life based on Bad's ill temper or Lady's Abernath's blackmailing attempts. I'm done." Then she snapped open the door and started down the steps, holding her dress, she made her way down out of the carriage.

Jack jumped up. "I'll talk with her," he said over his shoulder. "It's been a trying time for everyone."

Emily nodded. "I'll come too."

"We'll all go," Ada said as she slid down the bench, worrying her lip. "Grace is just tired of being at home and in need of a repose."

"Are you very angry with her?" Emily asked climbing out of the carriage.

Ada shook her head. "Not very. She's likely right."

"She isn't. You're being smart while she is acting rash." Vice reached out his hand and she placed her gloved one in his, warmth erasing some of her ill feeling. "Good for you for standing up to her. I know it wasn't easy but I'm proud—"

A scream made Ada stop moving mid-sentence, her foot perched on one step. Quick as a snake, Blake reached for her and pulled her into his arms as a shot rang out on the busy street.

More screams filled the air as Vice pressed her body against the carriage, using his much larger one as a shield.

Someone else yelled. Emily, letting out a low moan close by. "Jack!"

Ada pushed against Blake's chest but he held her tight. "Don't move, love," he said in a hushed whisper.

Was he serious? He wanted her to stay here with Emily yelling. Who in her family had been hurt? "Let me go," she gasped out, pushing again.

"Ada," he grated out in a clipped tone. "I can't have you hurt. Hold still."

She calmed and he slowly backed up, his head swiveling from side to side.

"Ada," Emily yelled again. "Grace is gone!"

———

DEEP, sickening dread filled Vice's chest as he pulled

back. Grace was nowhere to be seen, Jack lay in a crumpled ball on the ground, Emily perched over him. What the bloody hell had just happened?

"Grace?" Ada shrieked, finally breaking free of him and running toward Emily. She stopped, searching the street then swung back around to him. "We have to find her!"

Vice rushed to her side, but bent down over his friend. "Jack?" He knew she was right but he had to check on his friend first. He couldn't just leave him to die in the street.

Jack rolled over, blood oozing from his arm. "Went straight through. I'll be all right."

Emily pulled up her skirts and began to rip out sections of petticoat then wrapped them about his arm. "Oh my love," she said in a trembling voice. "I'm so sorry. I should have come home last night. I—"

"Emily," he whispered. "This is my fault."

Ada tugged on Vice's sleeve. "Which did Grace go?"

"That way," Jack pointed. "A man with a scarred face carried her off into a large carriage." He let out a low groan as he sat up. "It had a distinctive pattern on it of carved horses."

Vice grimaced. How would they find her now? He knew the man who'd taken her was Crusher. Of course Abernath had sent her newest lackey. But he wouldn't just take her back to his club.

Ada grabbed his arm, pulling him toward the carriage. He blinked, realizing she was right. "We have to go now," she said.

"What's happened?" Bad suddenly stood in front of him.

"Get in the carriage," he said, practically tossing Ada in as well, "I'll explain on the way." Then he turned back to Emily. "Can you handle Jack?"

Emily nodded. "Our doctor's office is just across the street. I'll take care of him."

Bad climbed in the vehicle and Vice in just after him. "Head down Faulk Street. We're looking for a carriage with carved horses."

"Yes, my lord," the driver called back.

Vice closed the door as the carriage started down the lane.

"What happened?" Bad asked again. "Where is Grace?"

"Gone," Ada said, her voice quivering.

"Gone?" The color drained from his face. "What do you mean gone?"

"Crusher," Vice answered, his own stomach pitching. "At least, I think. Jack said he saw a man with scars all over his face grab her."

"And you said a carriage with horses carved in it?" Bad slammed his fist into the wood frame. "That's Crusher all right. He's ridiculously proud of that carriage. Bought it from an indebted marquess years ago."

Vice inwardly winced as he assessed Bad. His face twisted in pain, his skin pale and his brow set low. "That's good. We'll recognize the carriage."

Bad hit the side of the vehicle again. "I shouldn't have left her."

Vice looked to Ada as she stared down at her clasped hands. He watched as a tear ran down her face, sliding from her dark lashes over her cheek as it wet several of her freckles. She drew in a ragged breath. "I told her not to come out today."

"Hey," the driver called. "You see a carriage with horses carved on it?"

"Just went over the London Bridge," A man yelled back.

"London Bridge?" Vice furrowed his brow.

Bad stood from his seat, swinging open the door. "I'm going up front with the driver. I'll be able to spot the carriage better."

"Now?" Ada's head snapped up. "While the carriage is moving?"

"I'll be fine." Bad waved a dismissive hand as he swung open the door.

"Be careful," Ada cried. "The last thing we need, Lord Baderness, is for you to be hurt too."

Bad paused. "After what I just did, you're concerned for me?"

Ada shook her head. "You're angry at Grace for being so thick-headed. Trust me, I am too."

Bad stared at her then looked at Vice. Vice gave a small shrug but his lips curled into a smile. "She's very generous of spirit."

Bad gave a single nod. "I can see that." Then he swung out from the carriage. "I see them," he cried. "They're paying the toll on the bridge."

Ada clutched his arm. "We have to hurry."

Vice stuck his head out too and sure enough, stopped on the bridge was a carriage with stallions carved into its doors that were intricately painted. "How are we going to get over the bridge quickly?" Vice asked. "We can't lose them now."

"Sir," Bad called. "I'll give you twenty pounds for your horse and saddle."

"What?"

"Twenty pounds. Buy a new one, pocket the rest."

"Deal," the man answered.

Bad looked back at them. "Keep up as best you can."

Ada was still clutching Vice's arm. "Please. Bring her back to us."

Bad nodded and hopped out of the carriage.

"What should I do, my lord?" The driver called.

With a look at Ada's determined countenance, his decision was easy. "Keep following that coach."

# CHAPTER THIRTEEN

ADA HAD NEVER BEEN MORE tired in her life and yet less likely to fall asleep. They'd been driving for hours. They'd caught sight of the carriage a great deal in the beginning of the chase. Enough to know she and Blake were chasing Grace on a road north. But it had been hours since they'd seen the vehicle. And there was no sign of Bad.

Her head ached nearly as much as her body as she snuggled in the crook of Vice's arm. At least her pillow was comfortable, though his muscles were a bit hard. She glanced up at him, his eyes open and staring into the dark. "You're awake."

"So are you," he said looking down as he softly stroked her cheek. "You should try to rest."

"I can't," she answered. "I keep thinking of Grace alone with strange people. What if they hurt her?"

What if they did worse? She touched her chest, her heart beating madly. She couldn't even say the words out loud.

"She's all right," he answered softly, drawing her closer. "First of all, the countess doesn't want to hurt her. She just wants her to expose Daring. At this point, I hope Grace agrees. We'll likely sell the club anyway." He sighed. "Bad and I will see to your reputation and Grace's while we find Abernath and give her the punishment she is overdue."

"Take care of our reputations?" Ada sat up then, her insides tingling with realization. "What does that mean?"

Vice sat up too. "It's the middle of the night, love. You never went home." He reached for her hand. "We have to get married, Ada."

Her mouth went dry. "You'd do that for me?"

"I already told you I would last night." He leaned over and kissed her cheek. "I meant it then and I mean it now."

Part of her jumped in excitement while another cringed with the realization that this marriage was not of the heart but born of necessity. "All right. We'll marry after we find Grace."

He shook his head. "Sweetheart, I haven't wanted to say this, but we're not going to find her. Bad is."

"But we've come all this way." Her insides twisted as tears sprang to her eyes.

Vice took both her hands in his. "Listen. We haven't seen any sign of the carriage. Not in hours. For all we know, they veered off the North road ages ago." He wrapped his arms about her, pulling her close. "I didn't want to give up either but Crusher's carriage is lighter and faster than this beast."

Ada shook her head. She couldn't give up on Grace. "But they'll have to stop eventually and we can catch up."

Vice pulled her into his lap. "Listen, love. Baderness is not like other lords. He grew up in the slums of London. He was a street fighter before he was a lord. The man never seems to tire. Never gives up and is tougher than the rest of us combined. If anyone is going to get Grace, it's him."

Ada couldn't help it. The tears she'd been holding back most of the day began to fall. She was tired and frightened and Grace was in so much danger. "I have to help find her, Blake. I'll never forgive myself."

He nodded. "I understand. We'll stop in the next town. We'll ask if anyone saw the carriage. Get food, change the horses."

"All right." Then she snuggled her tear-streaked face deeper into the crook of his neck. "Thank you for helping me."

"Ada," he crooned, his voice like a caress. "It's me who should be thanking you."

"For what?" she asked, lifting her head again.

He held her face in his hands. "For being so strong. They're wrong about you. You're not a frightened bird at all. You're thoughtful and careful but showing good sense is different than being afraid. Never forget that."

Those words filled her heart more than anything anyone had ever said to her. "Do you truly mean that?"

"Every word," he answered, then his lips captured hers.

She loved her cousin but Grace's barbs in front of everyone had cut her deeply and Blake's support now was like salve on a wound. As his lips moved over hers, she lost herself in that kiss. "You are one of the finest men I know."

He drew in a sharp breath, his hands holding her face tighter. "You don't have to say that. Agreeing to marry me was enough."

Her brow crinkled in question. "Have to say that? What do you mean?"

His face spasmed, his gaze casting down. "I'm named Vice. I told you, I was rejected by the first woman that I asked to marry me because of my loose morals. She said—"

"Stop." Ada understood but she didn't believe it. Not for a moment. "It's your turn to listen to me. She never looked deeper and that's her loss. Because underneath the practiced lines and the sky-blue eyes is a good man. The sort that saves women at parties, and launches overnight rescues, and marries a woman to save her reputation."

"So you're not sorry to marry me?" His voice shook as he searched her eyes with his own.

"Sorry?" She smiled warmly and then she leaned down to place a light peck on his lips. "I'm honored."

He closed his eyes, sagging deeper against her. "Swear to me that you mean it."

"I mean it," she replied, wrapping her arms about his neck.

Their bodies crushed together as he captured her mouth again, kissing her over and over. And when he slanted her lips open, she eagerly parted, ready for a taste of his tongue. They both groaned as the kiss deepened, growing more intense with each passing swipe of their mouth.

"Beg pardon, my lord," the driver yelled. "But we're approaching a village."

Slowly, Blake withdrew. "We'll stop," he called back.

All of Ada's worries that she'd managed to forget

for a moment came rushing back. "I hope this is the right decision."

"Me too," he replied. "But we'll have to put our faith in Bad."

———

Vice held Ada close as they exited the carriage. He needed her by his side because he was worried for her safety but also because he couldn't bear to be separated from her now.

He swallowed. Did she really mean what she'd said? His fingers tightened at her waist. Ada didn't lie.

If she were a different sort, he might weep for the joy of being at her side. How had he ever thought her less? She was more of everything. More love, more kindness, more beauty inside and out.

And she found him worthy? He couldn't quite believe it. The village was small, with a single inn and tavern and a small barn just to its left. The driver shuffled off to attend the horses while Vice headed toward the tavern's main door.

He glanced over at Ada. He'd told her that they'd stop for food but the truth was they should stop for the night. They had no idea which direction to travel and no chance of catching up to

Crusher. But he understood her need to not abandon her family.

The innkeeper glanced at the door, his eyes narrowing as Vice approached. How odd.

"Evenin'," the man called. "You wouldn't be Vice, would ye?"

That made him stop. "I am."

The man toddled over. "Mind if I ask what ye're chasin'?"

"Mind if I ask why you're asking?" Vice shifted Ada further behind him. How did this man know who he was?

"Dark fellow, referred to himself as Bad, said ye'd be comin'. Said ye'd look like an angel and ye'd have a redhead with ye. Left a message and a fat purse for me to deliver it to the correct man."

Vice relaxed a bit. "I'm chasing a carriage carved with horses. How long ago did he pass through?"

The other man gave him a delighted grin. "Yer the right one." Then he turned and started for the desk from which he pulled out a sheet of parchment. "He left about an hour ago. But he was only minutes behind the man yer lookin' for. Bad said to tell ye he'd have her back before the night was done and that ye should wait for him here." Then he handed Vice the sheet of paper.

Ada gasped, tugging on his arm. "Is he telling the

truth? Should we really wait? Perhaps we should follow in case he needs help or he fails. What if he fails?"

Vice skimmed the contents of the hastily scrolled letter. "He won't fail." His shoulders relaxed further. "He's intentionally fallen back so that Crusher thinks he's lost Bad. That way, Bad can launch a sneak attack." Then he handed Ada the letter.

Bad had been on them from the first moment. He'd tried to overtake the carriage but Crusher had a light and agile vehicle. He'd pretended to be wounded so that Crusher thought he'd have a chance at escape. What was more, Abernath was with them he was fairly certain, and she'd been hit by a ball of lead.

Ada gasped covering her mouth. "Oh dear. Lady Abernath's been shot."

"Can we have a table please, sir," Vice asked. "And two bowls of whatever stew you've got in the pot."

The innkeeper nodded, "Of course."

"I'll need parchment and ink as well."

"What for?" Ada asked, holding the paper in her hands.

"I have to write to your family. They need to know what's happening." He grimaced. "I should have just told your father what was going on to begin with. We wouldn't be in this mess if I had."

"But Daring—" She started.

"Daring was trying to protect the club." Vice dropped his cheek to the hair. "Which was a mistake all along. We should have said to hell with the club and worked harder to protect you."

She shook her head. "Diana told me that Exile uses the profits of the club to keep his lands in Scotland from sinking under debt and his people fed. You had good reason to protect that asset."

He looked at Ada, her soft green eyes shining back at him. They entered a private dining room and he helped her into a chair. "As usual, you are too kind."

She shook her head. "I'm not being kind, I'm being practical. You've talked of selling the club but some of the men depend on it, do they not?"

She had a point. "What do I say to your family?"

"Tell them the truth. Abernath kidnapped Grace. We're chasing after her. You intend to marry me to ensure my reputation is protected. Where are we? Abbotville?"

"Yes," he answered as he dipped the quill in the ink. "Anything else?"

"Tell them Bad is about to rescue Grace and we'll all," she drew out the word *all*, adding emphasis, "be home very soon. Also, remind them not to involve the Bow Street Runners. At this point, our reputations are more important."

He nodded, scratching the paper as he hastily penned the note. Once he'd finished, two bowls of steaming lamb stew arrived along with some bread, the innkeeper setting the bowls in front of them.

Ada sighed. "I am hungry."

"Of course, you are. We haven't eaten in hours." He folded his note and handed it to their host. "Would you be so kind as to see this letter delivered tonight?" Then he fished in his pocket and pulled out several coins.

"Of course, sir," the innkeeper answered, pocketing the money. "I've got just the boy for the job."

Vice nodded his thanks as the man left again. They both dug in, eating without speaking. He drew in a deep breath as he finished, his mind working far better. "Now," he said, looking across at his soon-to-be wife. "We need to discuss tonight."

She leaned forward. "We're going to continue on, aren't we?"

Vice shook his head. He hated to disappoint her now. She'd given him so much. "We'd never catch them, love."

Ada's face spasmed. "I want to help."

He reached for her hand. "I know you do but my job, here and now, is to protect you. Bad will keep

Grace safe. I can't leave you alone and I shouldn't take you any further."

Ada's voice shook as she spoke. "I don't want to leave her."

He squeezed her fingers. "But we tried, Ada. At this point, we're too far behind and we're at an actual crossroads. We don't even know which direction they've gone." He could see the pain on her face and his own constricted with a deep ache. He knew she was right. Bad could fail. But right now, he needed to keep the woman he loved safe. And he did love her.

This crazy night had taught him one thing, Ada Chase was the perfect woman for him. He would marry her and he'd spend his life cherishing the woman who effortlessly gave him so much.

## CHAPTER FOURTEEN

ADA LOOKED across the table at Blake. She knew he was right. But she hated to sit here and do nothing. "We've come this far," she murmured.

He leaned toward her. "And we'll be close enough to help if they send for us." He held her hand in his, his thumb massaging circles on spot sensitive skin between her thumb and forefinger.

She nodded, a shiver running down her spine. "What if she's hurt?"

Vice reached for her other hand. "I love that you are so concerned for others. But Ada, we have to think about you too." Then he stood, stepping around the table and pulling her up. "Just a few hours' sleep. You'll be better able to care for her when Bad rescues her if you're rested."

She gave an absent nod. He did have a point.

They returned to the desk but she barely paid attention as he spoke with the innkeeper then led her up the stairs. He unlocked a door and opened it for her, then followed her inside.

When he shut the wooden panel behind him, she realized he intended to stay. "Oh," she gasped, spinning about. "One room?"

He raised a brow. "I can sleep on the floor but after all that's happened today..." He cleared his throat. "I'm not leaving you alone."

Heat filled her cheeks. "That also makes sense. And I know we're about to be married..."

He crossed the room, drawing her against him. "Ada." He brushed a light kiss at her temple. "I'm just going to keep you safe. That's all."

Why were those words a bit...disappointing?

"I know. I just..." She didn't know quite what to say. "I somehow didn't picture my first night alone with a man to be like this."

He ran his finger down the side of her face. "This...exciting? Action-filled?"

That made her laugh, just a bit. "I suppose it has been all those things."

"I know you're worried about Grace but she is a tenacious woman and Bad..." Vice dropped his head closer. "I think he's in love with her. He won't admit it, even to himself. In his defense, we're a bit thick that way. But I am sure he's not going to allow anything to happen to her."

"Really?" Somehow those words did make her feel better. If Bad loved Grace, he'd move heaven and earth to protect her. "It has only just occurred to me that if this all works out then Bad's rescue might be rather romantic."

Vice gave a small chuckle. "It's a good thing neither of them are here to listen to that."

Ada's smile slipped.

He placed a soft kiss on her lips. "She's fine. If Bad is on her trail with a plan, he'll succeed, Ada. He's relentless." Vice had seen his friend take on men twice his size when he managed the floor of the club. He never got flustered or angry and he was strong, skilled, and shrewd. "There is no better man to help her."

"You're certain?"

He kissed her again, drawing her closer. She settled into the hollows of his body, like a puzzle fit together. So right. "I'm sure."

She wound her hands about his neck as he kissed her again and then again. She wore a light pelisse but he had the distinct urge to feel more of her and he slid his hands up her sides, easily pulling apart the buttons and sliding the coat down her arms. Tossing it onto the chair next to the bed, he drew her in again. "I'll help you undress, love. You'll sleep more comfortably."

She shook her head. "I don't think that's a good idea."

He pursed his lips, knowing he might have to beg. He'd be a gentleman, she was about to be his wife after all, but damn it all to hell, he needed to touch and feel a bit more of her. "I only mean to help."

Behind his head, he felt her undo the small buttons at the wrists of her gloves and then pull the fabric off her hands. Her fingers slipped through the strands of his hair. "I've never asked you, you don't have any siblings, do you?"

"No," he said, leaning into her touch. If she didn't stop soon, he was liable to forget his commitment to being a gentleman. "Just me. My parents died when I was thirteen and I've been alone ever since."

She stroked her fingers through his hair again, raking his scalp in the most pleasant way. "That must have been difficult."

"It was, honestly. But now I have you. And soon we'll have a family of our own." He closed his eyes, wishing to kiss her again.

"It's a pity some woman doesn't have this hair. So silky and the color is beautiful. Do you think we'll have a daughter with hair like yours?"

Discussing children, specifically the making of, nearly undid him. His body went rigid as a tree. "She'll have beautiful auburn hair, the color of the setting sun."

She gave a husky laugh, low and intimate. It made him shiver. "I hope not. Your hair is so much nicer."

He bent down and captured her lips again. He couldn't help himself. Not a kiss of comfort but a plea of passion. She met his touch with an equal amount of need. "Never say that," he whispered between kisses. "I told you from the beginning. Auburn is my very favorite shade."

She sighed into his lips and then kissed him, her tongue sliding along his bottom lips. "My dress is uncomfortable," she murmured. "Perhaps it would be better if you helped me undress after all."

———

ADA TOOK A STEP BACK, lacing her hands behind her to start working the buttons of her gown. She was certain of several key points. One, she was unlikely to sleep much. Both because of Grace and because she was now staying in a room with the only man that made her heart beat wildly in her chest. Two, they were getting married. "When do you think we'll have the ceremony?" she asked, undoing several buttons.

His eyes burned into her. "Tomorrow? The next day?"

She gasped, her hands pausing. "But the license?"

He stepped closer and continued the job of undoing her gown. "If you've enough money, it's easy to work around."

The bodice of her dress slumped forward and Blake began to carefully remove the fabric from her arms. Together, they shimmied the dress over her hips where it collapsed in a pool at her feet. His hands were achingly gentle as he bent to assist the dress, she ran her fingers through his hair. Something about his touch erased the fear she had inside. All she could feel with him close was excitement and comfort and...love. The word hit her like an actual blow. She loved him. Had loved him for some time, in fact. What had held her back was the fear he wouldn't return her affection.

He stood back up and pulled her tighter to him, his mouth finding hers again. They stood like that in the flickering flames of the fire, touching, kissing, as he unlaced her corset and she undid the buttons of his jacket.

"Blake," she said against his mouth. "I have to tell you something."

He paused, then pulled his head back. "What is it?" His voice was rough. Pained.

She swallowed. Would he rescind his offer if he knew of her feelings? Would she frighten her former rake away? "I… I meant what said when I told you that I thought you were the best sort of man. I know that you're marrying me out of duty, which I really appreciate."

One of his brows lifted and then he slid her hands from around her waist. Disappointment formed a ball of ache in her chest but then he reached for his cravat, loosening the knot. "I am not just marrying you out of duty."

"You're not?" she asked, licking her lips as she watched his fingers slide nimbly undoing the knot and pulling the fabric of his cravat from his collar. His shirt quickly followed suit and her mouth went dry as she assessed his chest. The muscles were deeply defined and she reached up her fingers to trail them along the ridges of his stomach.

"No, Ada. I am marrying you because you are the finest woman I've ever met. The kindest, and in your own way, the strongest."

"Strongest?" she gasped her heart surging.

He reached out and wrapped a hand about her neck, his fingers cradling the base of her skull. "You freely give love to anyone who needs it. That takes strength. A strength I didn't have until I met you." He grimaced then. "There have been other women. I'll tell you about them if you need to know."

"I don't." She shook her head then titled it to the side. "Are there any children that might be yours?"

That nearly made him smile. "Not that I'm aware of."

She nodded. "Any women who might be hatching plots of revenge?"

He did grin that time as he cupped her cheek with his other hand. "I don't think so."

"Then we're fine," She brought her other hand up to begin sliding both to his back, her fingers exploring the ridges and valleys within his muscles.

He sucked in his breath. "You're making it difficult to concentrate."

"Should I be sorry?" she asked and then she kissed his chest, pressing her delicate mouth to his skin. He clenched in need.

"I have to tell you this." Blake pulled her back. "None of those women can even compare to you, love. None of them could breach the walls I'd put up around my heart. Look at you. Grace was mean to you today. I might have railed and shook my fist at her and closed off my feelings but not you. Here you are, chasing after her with all the love you have. That takes a special person and I love who you are. I love you."

She gasped, going still. Had he really just said that? "You love me?"

"I do." He loosened the tie on her chemise. "It's all right if you don't feel the same. Your affection and consent to my proposal are enough. I just want to be with you, Ada."

Her heart nearly burst from her chest. He loved her? She didn't give him time to finish loosening her chemise, instead, she tossed herself at his chest, wrapping her arms about his neck. "Don't be silly. I love you too."

"Silly?" He laughed even as he crushed her body against his, lifting her feet from the floor. "Why would you want to love me I am—"

"What are you?" she asked, touching her nose to his. "Strong, protective, kind. How could I not?"

He swung her in a strong circle. "I'll do my best to take care of you always." He kissed her again. With so little clothing, she could feel the press of his body, the friction of his skin. Her breath caught as his tongue slid into her mouth.

He lay her down on the bed, his weight pressing on top of hers. He felt delicious…and she might have laughed at the word except for his kisses were stealing all reasonable thought from her brain.

Her chemise slid up her legs and his weight settled between them, the press of something hard rubbing against her sensitive flesh between her legs.

She moaned at the feel of it and without thought, shifted, only to find that friction increased the pleasure.

He reached a hand under her behind, tilting her hips even as he moved with her, causing a riot of pleasure to spread out from that single point all through her body.

With startling ability, he set a pace, seeming to know exactly how much pressure to put on her swollen flesh and exactly where and how to press.

Before she knew what was happening, her body tightened in pleasure, searching for some release she didn't entirely understand until she fell over the edge, her body seeming to shatter into a thousand tiny pieces.

# CHAPTER FIFTEEN

Tension, like a knot, pulled at every muscle in his body as Ada cried out her climax. In the beginning, he'd had lovely thoughts of only pleasuring her. Of saving their union for matrimony. But between her declaration of love and the sight and sound of her pleasure, he thought he might die if he had to wait any longer.

"Ada...love..." He could practically hear himself begging. "I want to..."

"Yes," she answered. "I want you too. All of you."

His cock throbbed as he stood, yanking at his boots despite the fact the damn things wouldn't come off. He nearly fell over from the effort. Not that this surprised him. Since the first, Ada had reduced him to a bumbling idiot. He'd managed to fall out of a chair, for pity's sake.

She stood too, then pushed him down onto the bed. He willingly flopped back as she bent down between his legs, working the boots off his body. Then, she slid her hands up his thighs and over his hips, reducing him to a throbbing nerve of need. His breath stalled in his chest when she reached for the falls of his breeches. "Shall I help you with these too?"

He blinked, unable to actually speak. He felt like a boy again, fumbling in his excitement while she was so calm and collected. "Are you afraid?"

She shook her head. Part of her hair had come undone and he wished to pull all the pins out but he didn't think himself capable tonight. "I'm with you. How could I be afraid?" And then she pulled down the pants, freeing his cock.

He held still and watched her inspect him. "It's larger than I thought."

"Is it?" he managed to say between breaths.

"Will it hurt?"

"At first," he answered grasping her hands and pulling her toward him. He wanted her but not if she worried. "We can wait. I don't want to—"

She kissed him into silence. "I don't want to wait. I just want to be prepared for you." Then she pulled away again, her chemise sailing over her head. In short order, her pantaloons followed suit, stockings and boots left in a pile. She stood before him stunningly naked. Round, high breasts and a tiny waist met his gaze, accentuated by the flare of her hips. And on her chest, a smattering of freckles.

"One day, I am going to kiss and count each of those freckles," he growled, sitting up to pull her back on top of him. She came willingly, her skin sliding along his. She was achingly soft and so silky he nearly came undone.

Grazing his hand along her back, he traced the ample curve of her behind and then slid his fingers into the crevice between her legs. She was wet and ready for him and he groaned again as her legs parted, spreading to either side of his hips.

He didn't even try, his cock just found her opening, pressing into the waiting folds. "I love you, Ada," he groaned even as he slid a little inside her.

With a decided push, she took all of him in, her maidenhead breaking in one quick motion. He heard her gasp of pain as she tightened. "I love you too. So much."

What a gift he'd been given. He wasn't certain what he'd done to deserve it but he knew, without a doubt, that he'd cherish her always. Lacing his fingers with hers, they stayed locked together, murmuring quiet words of love until she relaxed and he moved inside her, pulling out and then slowly pushing back in. She didn't tense in pain so he tried it again. Minutes passed as he gently quickened the pace allowing her body to adjust. Part of him wanted to seat himself fully inside her and unleash his passion but he had loads of chances for that. This was their first time together and he wanted every moment to be special.

He felt the shift in her. The moment that she relaxed and then began to enjoy their union. Moving faster, he reached a hand around her buttocks, making sure to apply pressure exactly where she'd need it.

Her low moan in his ear told him that he'd found the mark and he smiled a bit despite the numbing pleasure robbing him of reasonable thought. Then he couldn't think any more as they moved faster and faster, climbing toward the finish.

They crashed together, his body pressing into hers as he moaned her name one last time. "Ada."

Her spasms and low cries were her only response and then she collapsed on top of him. Rolling to the side, he managed to tuck them both under the covers and he'd swear, as the blanket settled over her body, she was already asleep.

Pulling her close to his chest, he closed his eyes and drifted away.

———

Ada wasn't certain the time, but she woke to a decided banging on the door.

"Forgive me sir, but there's a message for you," a gruff voice called.

Sir? She shifted, trying to force her mind to work. That's when her bottom pushed into the large, hard body behind her. Her eyes flew open.

"Give me minute," a deep sleepy voice rumbled behind her. "How long have we been asleep? An hour?"

Blake. She melted into his hard angles. A girl could get used to waking up like this. "I've no idea. I can't remember ever sleeping like that."

He chuckled but the sound was interrupted by another knock. "Sir, the delivery boy said it was urgent."

Urgent? Her eyes snapped open and she began to sit up, but Blake climbed over her, pushing her back down. "Don't move."

"But I have to move. We're going to rescue Grace this morning. You said after a few hours' sleep, we'd leave and—" But he slipped on his breeches and crossed the room. As he turned the lock, Ada buried herself under the covers.

"Yes?" Blake asked, his tone far more clipped.

"This just arrived for you." She heard the shuffle of parchment.

"Thank you," Blake answered and then the door clicked closed.

Ada popped back out from under the blanket. "Who's it from? What does it say?"

Blake was staring at the note. "It's from Bad."

Tucking the blankets about her chest, she sat up. Her fingers tingled with worried excitement. "And?"

Blake looked up from the sheet in his hand. "He says it's done."

Her fingers tightened on the blanket. "What's done? Grace's rescue? Crusher's capture? Lady Abernath's attacks? Is Grace safe? Should we follow, stay here, go home?"

Blake dropped the parchment next to her on the bed. She picked it up and read the four words scrolled out in scratchy block on the page.

*Vice,*

IT'S DONE.

*Bad*

. . .

SHE STARED at the words for a full minute as though she expected more answers to jump from the page. "You can't be serious," she finally mumbled. "This is it?"

"That's it." Vice climbed over her and slipped back into the covers. "We might as well go back to sleep."

"Sleep?" She turned to him outraged. "How can you even think about sleep? I need answers."

He sighed and reached for her waist, pulling her body against his. "Ada," he whispered. "I told you. Bad is taking care of Grace. Now, for heaven's sake, allow me to take care of you."

"I am cared for," she sniffed, leaning back to look at him. "I'm warm and in a bed with dinner from last night still in my stomach. I'm marrying a viscount and…" She held up a single finger. "I don't even have to have a wedding with my mother's interference."

He chuckled. "All excellent points. But think on this. If Bad didn't have Grace, he'd be here. He wouldn't have sent a messenger."

"Oh," she answered, placing her hand on his neck. "I hadn't thought of that."

"And if Crusher or Abernath were chasing them, he likely wouldn't have said that it was all done. He'd have called for my help."

"That…that is true too."

"So, I propose that you allow me to take care of you this morning, just for a few hours. We'll sleep a bit more, journey back to London, and see the Archbishop for a special license. With any luck, we can be married today."

"Do you think Bad will marry Grace?"

Blake shook his head. "We'll figure out how to protect Grace after I've taken care of you. But I am certain he'll keep her safe at all costs."

Ada turned her head to the side, assessing him. "You're very difficult to argue with this morning."

"It's my bare chest." He puffed his muscles, sucking in his stomach.

Ada had to hide a smile as she wrapped her arms about his middle. "I thought it was your sound arguments."

He leaned down, capturing her lips with his own. "I like the idea of my chest being the reason much better."

She would have argued but he kissed her again, his tongue sliding along the seam of her lips. As he slanted her mouth open, she forgot what she was going to say.

He rolled on top of her, tucking her body under his as he continued to kiss her. Last night had been a frenzy of passion but this morning, she wanted to explore.

She ran her hands over the ridges of his back, sliding them down to his muscular buttocks.

He made one of those growling sounds, the kind that gave her chills, his deep baritone vibrating in his throat.

"Love," he rumbled. "Touch me like that again and the pace is going to get a great deal quicker."

His words filled with deep satisfaction. The power she had over him intoxicated her. "Touch you how? Like this?" She slid her fingers to the inside of his thigh.

He groaned against her lips. "Don't say you didn't ask for this." And then he slid his body off hers, kissing a path over her jaw and down her neck.

As his hot kisses drew closer to her breast, the flesh puckered in anticipation, but nothing prepared her for the sensation of a damp mouth sucking in her flesh. Her entire body arched up to meet his lips, wanting more from him. He gave a throaty chuckle in response as he kissed his way to the other peak.

She wanted his touch so much, she used her hands to bring him closer, urge him toward the nipple.

"Hells bells, you're so beautiful, Ada." His thumb grazed the tender flesh before he sucked the other breast into his mouth.

She twisted her fingers through his hair, digging

deeper, the ache between her legs pulsing with need. As if he sensed that, he stroked his hand down her belly and then he cupped her mound, gently parting the soft flesh for his exploration.

Her vision blurred as bright colors danced before her eyes and need built inside her. Without meaning to, she found herself begging. "Please. Oh yes, there. Please."

For a moment he stopped, but then the velvety head of his manhood took its place. There was no pain this time, just delicious pleasure as he slid inside her, filling her with his hard length.

They moved together, slowly at first, but then building to amazing heights until they crashed over the edge together.

Ada, after having sworn she wasn't tired, felt her eyes drift closed. She pried them open again just in time to see the first rays of the sun peeking into the window. "Oh look. It's the start of the day."

Blake rolled to the side, tucking her against him. "The start of our wedding day, my love."

Oh dear. Butterflies flitted about her belly. That was exciting. Her eyes popped open again just as his closed. "You're not going to sleep, are you? It's too exciting to think about sleeping."

One eye popped open. "The church won't be open for a few hours at least."

"What does that have to do with being awake?" She poked his shoulder. "This might be the most wonderful day of my life."

Both his eyes opened then and he smiled tenderly. "Mine too." Then his grin turned wicked. "And I think I know how we can pass the time."

"Oh," Ada answered as his lips found hers again.

# EPILOGUE

WITH THE LIGHT OF DAY, and their very early start, their trip back to London was significantly shorter than their trip out had been.

Now it was before noon and they stood in front of the Bishop of Canterbury, special license in hand.

Ada held both of Blake's hands as they faced one another. She couldn't quite keep still as she beamed at the man who was about to be her husband. This was a dream come true. "I have to confess that I saw you once...getting cakes with an actress."

Blake's smile disappeared. "That woman meant nothing compared to you," he whispered as the bishop arranged candles.

She shook her head. "You misunderstand. You stole my breath that day and take it still now."

Blake pulled her closer, leaning his forehead against hers. The bishop looked up then.

Ada pressed her lips together. She'd had to assure the man that her family approved, that Blake was just rescuing her reputation after the dastardly deeds of Crusher and Abernath. Reluctantly, he'd agreed to the license and the rushed ceremony. Blake's generous donation had likely helped.

"And you mine," he answered. "We're ready to begin whenever you are, Your Grace."

"Wait," a feminine voice called from the back of the church. "Please wait."

Ada's head snapped up to see Diana and Exile rushing down the aisle, her mother and father just behind them. "You're here," she exclaimed.

"You said they approved," the archbishop rumbled.

"We do," her mother called, gasping for breath. "You're sure Grace is all right?"

Blake gave her hands a squeeze. "As soon as the ceremony is over, Exile and I will go find them and escort them home."

"What?" Ada asked. "You assured me that Baderness had this all well in hand."

Blake stepped a little closer. "He likely does. But

to be safe, I'll return. Just as I brought you back to London to make sure that you are all right."

"Why didn't you just leave me in London to begin with?" she asked, a ball of dread settling her stomach.

"I should have. Though I won't regret what has brought this moment about, love."

Those words softened her heart a bit. "I wanted to go."

He gave her a gentle smile. "I know."

Diana made it to the front of the church, standing just in front of them. "We're all returning to see that Grace is safe but I, for one, think you did the right thing, bringing Ada back here to marry."

"Thank you," Blake answered. "But Exile, tell your wife—"

"Nope," Exile answered before he could finish. "She's stronger than most men. I'll not tell her she has to stay home."

"Then I'm coming too." Ada straightened. "Grace might need us."

Blake gave a single nod. "Very well. Your Grace, if you'd be so kind as to see us wed, we're returning to the country tonight on a rescue mission." Then he winked. "Jack's driver will rue the day he picked us up."

Years later, Ada couldn't remember the details of

the ceremony. What she wore, the exact words she said. But the feeling would stay with her forever. Warmth surrounded her. She'd found a man who valued her for who she was and even better, he brought out the very best in her.

"I could never ask for more than you, Lord Viceroy."

Blake placed a soft kiss on his wife's mouth. "And I never dreamed to earn the love of a woman such as you, Lady Viceroy."

Her heart thrummed in her chest. "I'm ready to be my best self. Let's go find Grace."

BARON OF BAD
Lords of Scandal Book 5

Tammy Andresen

# BARON OF BAD

Lady Grace Chase gripped the side of the carriage with increasingly stiff fingers as she eyed the pale-faced blonde woman who sat across from her.

Lady Cristina Abernath held a long dagger in her thin hand as she stared back at Grace. "It didn't have to be this way."

Grace parted her lips to reply, but hesitated. She wasn't the most sensible woman in England. In fact, of her three sisters and two cousins that she'd grown up with, she might be the least intelligent of the bunch. But she knew, instinctually, when it was best to keep quiet. And now was one of those times.

Not that she always listened to her instincts. A few hours prior, she'd ignored her feelings entirely and stomped out of the carriage after she'd had a rather heated disagreement with the Baron of Baderness.

He'd accused her of being spoiled and she'd stormed off because of what he'd said, which of course, had allowed her to be kidnapped right in the middle of a busy London Street. If he were here now, she'd smack him, or hug him.

Maybe both.

"If one of your family could have just agreed to help me, I wouldn't have to take these measures. And then you went and stole my Harry too."

This time, words burned on the tip of Grace's tongue but she held them in. Accusations like Abernath had chosen to abandon the child in a locked room during a fire or that she'd stolen her sister, Cordelia, and attempted to take her other sister, Diana, recently. Instead, Grace tightened her hold on the wooden rail that trimmed the interior. It was a lovely carriage. She took in the rich red drapery and the shining mahogany of the interior. What an odd prison she was now held in.

"We can still make a deal. Tell me you're the most rational of the Chase women."

"Hardly," Grace murmured without meaning to. "But I'm willing to talk." Grace was by no means the most rational, which was likely a good thing. Cordelia was far more sensible for example. But that wouldn't help her in this situation. Abernath was completely off her rocker.

Rather than relaxing, Abernath tensed, narrowing her gaze. "One of your sisters already made that promise. I'm not sure I trust your word."

Grace shrugged, feigning indifference. She was being held at knifepoint in a carriage that was barreling down a country road with a scarred giant of a driver. Blood rushed through her ears. But she was the one who shouldn't be trusted? "I'm sure Diana made you promises. If I'm not mistaken, she likes you." That wasn't entirely true. Diana was the oldest daughter of the Earl of Winthorpe and the boldest of the bunch. She'd likened herself to Abernath, saying that she understood the countess's struggle. Being a strong woman, she'd been trapped into a corner by society.

Abernath, if Grace understood the story correctly, had cheated on her fiancé, the Duke of Darlington. He'd ended the engagement but the countess had been pregnant and married the Count of Abernath out of necessity.

"Likes me?" Lady Abernath lowered the knife a bit. "I'm not foolish enough to believe that."

Grace swallowed a lump while fisting up her skirts with her free hand. Perhaps she should have stayed silent. While stolen away, she was at least in one piece and she'd prefer to remain that way. She took a long breath. "Diana takes on the world with a strength and fight I could never imagine. Sometimes it's a great asset, other times, it makes her life infinitely more difficult. I suppose like is the wrong word. Kinship might be the better choice."

Abernath slumped back against her seat, the dagger dropping to her knee. "That does sound as though it could be true." Her face was frighteningly pale. "Can I tell you something?"

Grace leaned forward. "Of course." Her breath was coming in short gasps and her eyes widened but she kept her voice calm.

Abernath looked out the window. "I'm dying."

Her confession sent Grace back in her seat. "I beg your pardon?"

"Not even Crusher knows." And she nodded toward the front of the carriage. Grace could only assume he was the frightening driver.

"Are you shivering?" Grace asked, her gaze narrowing.

"Never you mind," Abernath snapped. "Daring owes me for what he did to my life."

The woman was vacillating wildly, which made Grace more afraid than any other part of this experi-ence. Her insides churned with fear as she pressed back into her seat. She held out her hands in front of her, making soft shushing noises. "I understand. He hurt you."

Abernath nodded. Then, amazingly, she set the blade to the side and began pulling off her gloves. Grace sat silently transfixed, wondering what might be happening.

The moment the first glove came off, Grace had to gulp down her cry. Abernath's hands were covered in angry welts. "Oh dear," she whispered, not sure what else to say. She looked into the woman's eyes, which were glassy and unfocused. "Do they hurt?"

Slowly Abernath leaned forward, holding herself as she rocked. "Try to understand," she whispered. "They went away and now, they've come back." The woman shook like a leaf. "I didn't want to hurt anyone, not you and not your sisters, but men won't help me. Men are the problem, not the solution. Even my son—" She stopped. "I've never had female friends but I need someone to aid me now."

Grace swallowed. "Men are the problem? Sometimes I think I know what you mean." She thought back to her fight with Bad. She didn't understand it at all. First, he wasn't that handsome. His nose was crooked and his skin was craggy. Well, he was dark and mysterious, and there was something powerful in his every movement and gesture, a confidence that seemed to radiate from within. Like he could handle anything.

But truly handsome, he wasn't. And she'd thought that meant she wasn't really interested in his attention. That was to say, she liked almost all attention but it didn't need to be his.

And he'd been attentive, if she were honest. But that was more because his friends had required him to be so. And perhaps that bothered her too. He should be spending time with her because he wanted to. She was attractive. Some even called her beautiful, and she was fun, she tried to be. But he'd yelled at her today, called her spoiled and selfish and…and she'd give anything to see his hard, dark face right now. Because if he were here, he'd surely make her feel as though everything was all right.

And then she could smack him for making her storm off like that.

"You haven't had a life like mine. I can see it in the sweet expression on your face. Your father, he was kind to you and I bet he didn't take advantage…" Her voice trailed off as she pressed her welted hands together. "Sometimes I think they've driven me mad. Or perhaps it's whatever is inside me causing this." And she held up her hands again.

Grace licked her dry lips. "You're not mad. Just… desperate." The woman was completely insane but again, it didn't seem prudent to say so. Then she swallowed. "So, you're worried you won't be with us for long. I understand. What do you need my help with?"

Abernath scooted forward, her eyes wide and wild. "Announce that Daring owns a share of the Den of Sin club. Force him to be public about his dual life. Then he can know some of my pain."

Grace took a deep breath. She'd heard of Abernath's affliction before, though she didn't know the name. The welts were thought to be caused by a weak constitution, especially when they were accompanied with madness. Was that the reason the woman was so unstable or was it her past? "I understand. He hurt you and now you want to make him pay." Her heart hammered in her chest. Was there any point in reasoning with a suffering woman? "But I'd like to ask you a question. Besides your personal satisfaction do you have another goal in mind with your plan? Is there something you hope to accomplish?"

Abernath gave her a sidelong glance. "I..." She pressed her hands together and then winced, setting them in her lap. "I need money."

Grace started to frown but then caught herself. Money? That wasn't madness, that was greed. While less dangerous it was somehow less satisfying as well. "So, you want me to help you blackmail the Duke for money?"

Abernath's face twisted. "I want you to help me provide a future for my son."

Grace's stomach dropped. When Abernath had kidnapped her sister, the house had caught on fire. Abernath had fled, leaving an ill-kept child in the house. Her sister and her new husband had adopted the child knowing he could never return to Abernath. Now the crazy woman wanted to provide for him? Grace couldn't believe it was true.

———

Benjamin Styles, as he'd been called the first twenty years of his life, rode the horse he'd absconded from a passerby as fast as the tired animal would go, which was not all that fast. The Baron of Baderness —it still amazed him that he'd acquired that title— hadn't seen the carriage he'd been chasing in almost an hour.

His stomach clenched in fear. He couldn't lose Grace now. How could he ever go home and face her family, his friends, if he lost the woman he'd been assigned to protect? How could he face himself?

Leaning out over the animal's neck, he urged the beast to go faster. He prided himself in being a man of honor. Even in a world often mad with greed and lust, he tried to hold his head above all the riff raff and conduct himself in a manner befitting his title.

Sure, he ran a gaming hell that fed men's worst afflictions. First, he believed that was their vice, not his. And second, he amended that as a former street urchin, he was particularly suited to keep the peace in such an establishment. In fact, he liked to think he kept all those men safer for his efforts. If not for his club, they'd likely participate in the same behaviors at another place. And that place would not have a man who'd acquired his particular set of skills.

Fear pulled at his chest. Though, one other man did possess his skill set, almost exactly. Crusher was the only name he'd ever known the man by. They'd been fighters together and now they owned rival clubs.

He'd never liked the man—a big, mean, dumb fellow with a giant chip on his shoulder about his success. And now he'd taken the most beautiful woman in all of London.

Bad could confess, at least to himself, that the sight of Grace made every muscle in his body tense and his breath stall in his throat. Why did he have to be so attracted to her? It complicated everything.

But his thoughts focused once again on her rescue. He'd worry about his bloody feelings later.

The carriage came into view, rumbling ahead of him as it bounced along the road. The sun glistened off polished wood, the distinctive pattern of carved horses flashing in the light.

Who used a carriage like that to stage a kidnapping? Not that Bad was complaining. It made tracking them exceptionally easy. Even the one time the carriage had nearly lost him, multiple passersby had been able to point him in the direction of the vehicle.

In Bad's opinion, the choice of carriage highlighted both Crusher's arrogance and stupidity. He'd enjoy making that man suffer when he got Grace back.

Crusher turned back from his seat and caught sight of Bad. Bad watched, his muscles clenching, as Crusher reached across the seat and then lifted a pistol from next to him on the seat and leaned back to fire.

The blast filled the air. Bad ducked low over the horse as a ball of lead whizzed by him. He had two choices, fall back again and wait until they surely stopped or surge ahead.

Just then, Abernath leaned out a carriage window, also holding a pistol in her hand.

She leveled the gun toward him. Bad pulled the pistol from his own waistcoat and fired at the same moment she did. Burning pain whizzed through his leg. And he looked down to see blood oozing down his pants. Still, he also noted the wound was on the fleshy exterior of his thigh.

Abernath, however, let out a scream and ducked back in the carriage. Not a moment later another scream cut the air. Cold dread washed through him. Grace.

Want to read more? Viscount of Vice
Also on this series:
Lords of Scandal
Duke of Daring
Marquess of Malice
Earl of Exile
Earl of Sin

## ABOUT THE AUTHOR

Tammy Andresen lives with her husband and three children just outside of Boston, Massachusetts. She grew up on the Seacoast of Maine, where she spent countless days dreaming up stories in blueberry fields and among the scrub pines that line the coast. Her mother loved to spin a yarn and Tammy filled many hours listening to her mother retell the classics. It was inevitable that at the age of eighteen, she headed off to Simmons College, where she studied English literature and education. She never left Massachusetts but some of her heart still resides in Maine and her family visits often.

Find out more about Tammy:
http://www.tammyandresen.com/
https://www.facebook.com/authortammyandresen
https://twitter.com/TammyAndresen
https://www.pinterest.com/tammy_andresen/
https://plus.google.com/+TammyAndresen/

Read Tammy Andresen's other books:

Seeds of Love: Prequel to the Lily in Bloom series

Lily in Bloom

Midnight Magic

*Keep up with all the latest news, sales, freebies, and releases by joining my newsletter!*

*www.tammyandresen.com*

*Hugs!*

OTHER TITLES BY TAMMY


**Chronicles of a Bluestocking**

Earl of Dryden

Too Wicked to Woo

Too Wicked to Want

Too Wicked to Wed


**How to Reform a Rake**

Don't Tell a Duke You Love Him

Meddle in a Marquess's Affairs

Never Trust an Errant Earl

Never Kiss an Earl at Midnight

Make a Viscount Beg


**Wicked Lords of London**

Earl of Sussex

My Duke's Seduction

My Duke's Deception

My Earl's Entrapment

My Duke's Desire

My Wicked Earl

**Brethren of Stone**

The Duke's Scottish Lass

Scottish Devil

Wicked Laird

Kilted Sin

Rogue Scot

The Fate of a Highland Rake

**A Laird to Love**

Christmastide with my Captain

My Enemy, My Earl

Heart of a Highlander

A Scot's Surrender

A Laird's Seduction

**Taming the Duke's Heart**

Taming a Duke's Reckless Heart

Taming a Duke's Wild Rose

Taming a Laird's Wild Lady

Taming a Rake into a Lord

Taming a Savage Gentleman

Taming a Rogue Earl

**Fairfield Fairy Tales**

Stealing a Lady's Heart

Hunting for a Lady's Heart

Entrapping a Lord's Love: Coming in February of 2018

**American Historical Romance**

Lily in Bloom

Midnight Magic

The Golden Rules of Love

**Boxsets!!**

Taming the Duke's Heart Books 1-3

American Brides

A Laird to Love

Wicked Lords of London

Printed in Great Britain
by Amazon